THE FIRST RULE OF CLIMATE CLUB

Also by Carrie Firestone
Dress Coded

ACKNOWLEDGMENTS

I owe a planet of gratitude to my editor, Stephanie Pitts, for guiding me, draft after draft, as we both got to know this club of characters. Thank you to the outstanding Putnam book whisperers, including but not limited to Jen Klonsky, Matt Phipps, Cindy Howle, Misha Kydd, Ariela Rudy Zaltzman, Elizabeth Johnson, Jacqueline Hornberger, Suki Boynton, Cindy De la Cruz, Danielle Ceccolini, Olivia Russo, and the stellar sales and marketing teams. And special thanks to Tyler Feder for making cover art that truly brings these characters to life.

Sara Crowe, I'm so glad you're my agent and friend. Thank you and the Pippin team for always knowing where to go and how to get there.

A lot of people helped inform, review, and inspire this book. Special thanks to Kamora Herrington; LaShantee Crawley; Meimouna Thioune; Brynna Morris; Kavya Jain; Kahrisma James; Martha Klein; Laura and Fiona Radmore; the network of PANS/PANDAS parents who are shedding light on this underdiagnosed syndrome; Tanya Contois; Dr. B (the original Dr. H); and Jennifer and Andrew Snyder, the bravest duo I know.

Thank you, teachers and librarians, especially my dear

friend Lisa Levinger, for finding creative ways to impart the gift of reading. I hope you all see a little bit of yourselves in the Fisher Middle School staff.

Eleni Kavros DeGraw, you are such a brilliant leader. You certainly would have inspired Ms. Lane, just like you inspire me with your kavorka every day. And thank you, Lucas DeGraw, for being the kind of kid the whole climate club would want to hang out with.

Thank you to my family, friends, and writer colleagues (especially my Pandas critique group) for enthusiastically supporting my work. Your cheers lift me up, and I love you all. Writing a book during a global pandemic had its challenges, but my "pod" made everything so much better. Thank you, Emily and Lauren Firestone and Lindsay Snyder, my original fairy finders; Michael Firestone, my best friend; and Roxie, the sweetest dog in the world.

Most of all, I want to thank the climate scientists, environmental justice activists, and ordinary people across the world who are stepping up and taking real action to address climate change and racial inequity in our lifetime. Let's grow this club together.

THE FIRST RULE OF CLIMATE CLUB

CARRIE FIRESTONE

putnam

G. P. PUTNAM'S SONS

G. P. PUTNAM'S SONS

An imprint of Penguin Random House LLC, New York

First published in the United States of America by G. P. Putnam's Sons,
an imprint of Penguin Random House LLC, 2022

Visit us online at penguinrandomhouse.com

Library of Congress Cataloging-in-Publication Data
Names: Firestone, Carrie, author.
Title: The first rule of Climate Club / Carrie Firestone.
Description: New York: G. P. Putnam's Sons, 2022. | Summary: When twelve-year-old
Mary Kate joins a special science pilot program focused on climate change, she and
her friends come up with big plans to bring lasting change to their community.
Identifiers: LCCN 2021049154 (print) | LCCN 2021049155 (ebook) |
ISBN 9781984816467 (hardcover) | ISBN 9781984816474 (epub)
Subjects: CYAC: Schools—Fiction. | Podcasts—Fiction. |
Environmental protection—Fiction. | Climatic changes—Fiction. | LCGFT: Fiction.
Classification: LCC PZ7.1.F55 Fi 2022 (print) | LCC PZ7.1.F55 (ebook) | DDC [Fic]—dc23
LC record available at https://lccn.loc.gov/2021049154
LC ebook record available at https://lccn.loc.gov/2021049155

Book manufactured in Canada

ISBN 9781984816467
1 3 5 7 9 10 8 6 4 2

FRI

Design by Suki Boynton & Cindy De la Cruz
Text set in Adobe Garamond Pro

For the unlikely problem solvers
The ones who build community
The ones who heal the planet

THE FIRST RULE of CLIMATE CLUB

THE LETTER THAT STARTS IT ALL

Dear Parent or Guardian,

I am pleased to announce that Fisher Middle School has received a generous grant to fund a climate science pilot program this year. The class will explore how and why climate change is happening and how we can use community-based projects to take action.

Out of over a hundred application essays students submitted in March, the following rising eighth graders have been selected to participate:

Elijah Campbell
Shawn Hill
Benjamin Lettle
Andrew Limski
Jay Mendes
Rabia Mohammed
Mary Kate Murphy
Lucy Perlman
Rebecca Phelps
Hannah Small

Warning! This class will be a lot of work. Please

talk to your child and make sure they're ready to commit. We will still cover standard eighth-grade science concepts, but this class is not going to be "traditional." If you and your child are on board, please sign and return the attached form. Congratulations to all the students!

I can't wait to get started.

Scientifically yours,
Ed Lu

THE FAIRY-HOUSE VILLAGE

My climate-class acceptance letter is stuck to the refrigerator door with an E magnet, next to a picture of my new baby niece, Penelope, and a Post-it reminding Dad to buy more back-pain cream.

All the inspirational E magnet words aren't working for me right now, because I'm not *eager* or *enthusiastic* or *excited* about school starting tomorrow. My best friend, Lucy, has been sick the whole summer, and nobody knows what's wrong with her. I would have been eager, enthusiastic, and excited to be in the climate class with Lucy. Instead, I'm going to be sitting with a group of kids I barely know.

I text Lucy: Fairy village? But she doesn't text back, which means she's sleeping, having a really sick day, or mad at me for even asking.

I'm almost thirteen years old, and I'm going to build a fairy house by myself. But Lucy and I promised each other we would do it every year the day before school starts, for good luck, and we really need the good luck right now. So I put on my shoes, call my dogs, Murphy and Claudia, to come with me, grab my backpack, and walk out the side door.

My backyard and Lucy's backyard are separated by a huge nature preserve, which was donated to our town by a family who must have had a crystal ball and seen that if you don't specifically say *This piece of land can never be used for anything but enjoying nature*, it will eventually turn into a Dunkin' Donuts, a car dealership, or a nail salon.

Not many people visit the preserve, probably because there aren't really trails. It's one huge chunk of beautiful land, with a sledding hill, and a meadow, and a pond, and a vernal pool in spring, and crumbling old stone walls, and woods surrounding it all.

I walk around our barn, which is now a big garage with an upstairs room, follow the path through the woods to the top of the sledding hill, and cut through the sunflowers at the edge of the meadow.

Most people wouldn't notice the fairy village if they made their way into the woods. It looks like some creature randomly dropped piles of bark and twigs. But we know. Lucy and I and the fairies have a lot of secrets hidden here.

When we were younger, we spent entire days collecting pine cones, and lost feathers, and interesting stones, and acorns, and fallen flower petals. We built fancy fairy houses and did all kinds of fairy-summoning rituals I can't remember anymore. But I don't feel like doing any of that. Right now, I want to build a house, get the good luck, and go home.

I pick up a few sturdy sticks and lean them against a fallen trunk that's covered in moss. I leave a space for the fairies to come and go, and cover the little lean-to with soft pine needles. I drop stones around the house and scatter handfuls of leaves on the roof.

It's not our best house, but it's good enough.

Sleep well, fairies, I wish. *And please bring us luck.*

My neighbor Molly and I have been sitting together on the bus since I was in kindergarten and she was in first grade. We used to get harassed by Molly's older brother, Danny, who calls us Frog and Toad for some reason, but Danny is living with his grandma in New York, so Frog and Toad have a break this year.

"Do you like my tank top?" I ask, sliding into the seat across from my other neighbor Will.

"I *love* your tank top," Molly says. "It really emphasizes those shoulders."

"Thank you, my queen," I say, because I'm very grateful that Molly and her friends started a protest against our school's dress code this past June, which ended with the school district letting us wear pretty much whatever we want.

"Remember how scared you were when school started last year?" Molly says, eating a granola bar. "I thought you were going to throw up."

"I wasn't looking forward to seventh grade."

What Molly doesn't know is that I wasn't scared. I was annoyed. I didn't know how I was going to go from an entire summer of frogging and tree climbing to being pushed down a crowded hallway eight times a day.

"I'm going to miss seeing you," Molly says. "Now I'm the one about to throw up. The high school has way too many people I don't know. Say something to distract me."

"Like what?"

"I don't know. Tell me about the podcast. Are you still going to do it?"

"I doubt it."

"Why not? It was really good."

I don't feel like talking about *Bearsville* with Molly. It's embarrassing.

Will shoves his phone in our faces to show us his summer-camp girlfriend, and Molly spends the rest of the bus ride asking him questions he doesn't know the answers to.

"Do you think you'll see her before next summer?"

"I don't know."

"Is she going to camp next summer?"

"I don't know."

The bus stops in front of the high school, and Molly makes an *ughhh* sound.

"You've got this, Molls," I say. "You're a queen, remember?"

Will and Molly jump off the bus, and Molly runs over to her friends Navya and Bea. I watch them go into the high school as the bus rolls out of the circle toward the first day of eighth grade.

FAILURE TO LAUNCH

I tried to start a podcast this summer. It was called *All's Well in Bearville*, but I changed it to *All's Well in Bearsville* after the first episode because there's a lot more than one bear in this town. It was supposed to be about why bear hunting in our state is inhumane, and how to deal with climate change, and interesting nature stories.

The *Bearsville* idea came from Molly, who used a podcast to start the dress-code protest, and then *Dress Coded: A Podcast* ended up inspiring people all over the country to fight their school dress codes.

Bearsville, on the other hand, never really went anywhere.

Maybe it was because the state had already passed a law banning bear hunting, or because the people I interviewed used a lot of science words. My cousin in Florida said the interview with the professor about climate change and frogs was "kind of boring." My other cousin said the questions I asked the tree expert were "too smart." Molly said, "It's really well done, Mary Kate, but people have a lot going on in the summer."

One of my mom's regular customers at the bookstore looked at the *Bearsville* flyer on the bulletin board and said, "I'm more of a book person than a podcast person."

The only people who actually listened to all three episodes were my ninety-one-year-old grandmother and her roommate, Linda, in Florida, and Lucy, who gave me a lot of content ideas.

Then Lucy got sick, I got distracted, and it was easy to let go of something that had only three listeners. It might have been different if I could have actually interviewed the bears, the frogs, and the trees.

Lucy texts right as the bus is turning down the long Fisher Middle School driveway: **On the way to another 'ologist. Come over after school. Good luck.**

LUCY AND THE 'OLOGISTS

Lucy started acting strange at the end of school last year.

At first, I thought she was mad at me. Every time I asked her to meet at the pond, she said she didn't feel good and needed to take a nap. Then I was afraid she was getting sick of me, or that she maybe wanted to go hang out with her basketball friends. But then I heard my mom on the phone with her mom.

"Have you tested her for anemia?"

"What about blood sugar issues?"

"I mean, narcolepsy, but the symptoms don't add up."

"Why would she think her food was contaminated? That's so odd. You're right. It does sound like anxiety."

It got worse. Every time I went to her house, all she wanted to do was sleep. Then she felt better for a while, at least good enough to go down to the pond one afternoon and wait for the bats to come out. Lucy is obsessed with bats. But even then, her legs hurt, and she had shooting pains in random places and squishy sounds in her ears and blurry vision and a burning tongue. And she was constantly worried about bugs getting in her mouth, so she didn't want to talk.

"I'm going home to sleep a little," she said. "I'll be back for the bats."

She was never back for the bats.

Lucy went to a psychiatrist (a mental health doctor) because she doesn't want to do anything or talk to anyone, and she's not herself *at all*. They gave her anxiety medicine that hasn't helped.

She went to a neurologist (a brain doctor) because she's forgetting words and now she has a thing where she jerks her arms and blinks her eyes over and over again.

Then a gastroenterologist (a stomach doctor) because onions and milk and a lot of other foods make her nauseated.

And a rheumatologist (a joint doctor) because her whole body hurts.

Nobody knows what's wrong with Lucy.

Today she's going to a urologist. She doesn't know that I know, but I overheard my mom talking to her mom again. It's scary and embarrassing, and I'll never tell anyone, but Lucy has been wetting the bed.

Before the last 'ologist appointment, Lucy said, "No matter what, Mare, I'm going to school. I'm not making you walk into that place alone."

That was a week ago. "No matter what" has come and gone.

THAT PLACE

"That place" is Fisher Middle School, which seems smaller today, for some reason.

The bus stops in front of the school, and I catch up with Talia, who is sitting a couple rows in front of me, before getting off. Then we follow everyone to the Kindness Garden, where Fisher students drop rocks with inspiring words painted on them before they start seventh grade. My word was so boring, I don't even remember it.

The new superintendent, Dr. Eastman, bursts out of the office wearing a black jumpsuit and yellow high heels and carrying a LET'S MAKE MAGIC THIS YEAR sign. She has strong witch vibes, and I like it.

She introduces our new principal, Ms. Singh, who has smiled more in the past three minutes than our old principal did in a year.

"Dr. Eastman seems so nice," Talia says. "I like her Southern accent."

Talia was part of the dress-code protest last year, which a lot of people think was the thing that drove out the old principal and his sidekick, a woman we called Fingertip. I'm pretty sure they're right.

"And this, friends, is Mr. Joe, our new dean of students," the superintendent says, putting her hand on Mr.

Joe's shoulder. "Is somebody giving you a hard time? Are you having a tough interpersonal issue? If so, go to Joe."

I give Talia a good-luck hug, find my locker, then walk to gym, where we introduce ourselves and say one thing we did over the summer: "I'm Mary Kate Murphy, and I visited my sister, Sarah, in Boston and met my new baby niece, Penelope." In math, we throw a ball of yarn around the class and have to say a fun fact about ourselves when we catch it. Wow. Now I know Ben Lettle's favorite color is brown.

I'm on my way to English when I run into big block letters that say CONGRATULATIONS TO OUR CLIMATE CLASS FOR THESE WINNING ESSAYS. Somebody thought it would be a good idea to hang our climate-class application essays on a bulletin board. Now the whole school can read about my weirdness whenever they walk by.

CLIMATE CLASS APPLICATION ESSAY

MARY KATE MURPHY

We always hear about climate change and polar bears, and that's very upsetting and devastating because polar bears are starving to death and turning to cannibalism. But I want to talk about the bears that live in my backyard.

Most people don't realize how many bears live in the middle of Connecticut. Our town has more bears than nearly any other town. I observe them all the time, especially a few different families that have been coming around for a while.

When I was little, the bears would always feed in this area of the Honey Hill Preserve that had a lot of wild blackberry bushes. I'm only twelve, but just in my lifetime I've seen the bushes ripening earlier and earlier with fewer and fewer berries. The bears have to look for other sources of food, and that means they are going to garbage cans and ending up on Facebook posts with people complaining about how annoying the bears are, which makes people want to start shooting them.

If you do an online search of nearly any plant or animal on Earth and then "climate change impact," you'll see ways entire ecosystems are being disrupted by climate change. But I don't need to look it up because I see it with my own eyes, with blackberries, bears, salamanders and frogs, plants and bees and butterflies. I'm not exaggerating. It's all changing every year.

If you accept me into the climate class, I would like to learn more about the changes I'm seeing in my backyard and how to stop them before all the creatures I actually care about are gone, because I consider these creatures my friends.

THIRD PERIOD

I'm still trying to get used to having only eight students in English class. There was a problem with the schedule, and now the people in my English class third period are the same people in my climate class eighth period. There's supposed to be ten of us, but Lucy is sick and Andrew Limski was forced to drop out of the pilot program because, according to Jay, his parents didn't think the climate class sounded challenging enough.

I watch everyone come in and sit in the circle of desks.

Ben Lettle grew a half mustache over the summer. Maybe his parents don't think he's ready to handle a razor. I get it. The bathtub scene whenever I try to shave my legs looks like the time Dad tried to blend tomatoes and forgot to put the top on the blender.

Elijah Campbell is wearing a bumblebee bow tie.

Shawn Hill grew, like, a foot since seventh grade and got glasses.

Rabia Mohammed's wearing the shoes I wanted, but Dad said what he always says: "That's too steep for our budget."

Jay Mendes has a green bruise on his forehead from playing soccer. (That was his fun fact in math.)

Hannah Small and Rebecca Phelps are whispering. This is eighth-grade code for *We hung out together at the pool club over the summer, and now we have secrets.*

Our English teacher, Ms. Lane, takes attendance. Ms. Lane has always been just Charlotte to me. She was one of the first people on earth I ever met. She and my sister, Sarah, who happens to be eighteen years older than me, have been best friends most of their lives, and Sarah brought Charlotte to the hospital after I was born to meet me.

"Today we begin our letter-writing project," Ms. Lane says.

"Seriously? Pen pals again?" Elijah says. "They literally never write back."

"No, not pen pals, Elijah." She goes to her desk, pulls a folded piece of yellow lined paper from her bag, and starts to read:

Dear Charlotte,

I really miss summer vacation. Ms. Milholland is making us write letters to ourselves, which seems weird, but whatever. She says she's not going to read the letters and they're for us to keep and read when we grow up. I trust her. She's pretty cool. I'm making an announcement that I haven't even told Sarah. I think I'm in love with Greg Johnson. Like, he's as perfect as a boy can be. He's got dimples, and he's taller than me. He's kind of like Leonardo DiCaprio from Titanic, *but hotter. Why does he have to be sixteen? Why is life so unfair? Bell ringing.*

Love
Me

We stare at her.

"That, my friends, was classic Ms. Lane in eighth grade. And I'm sharing it with you because, as embarrassing as it is, I adore these letters. I should also point out there's no comma between 'Love' and 'Me,' which is a good example of how a comma changes everything."

"Oh, I get it," Rebecca says, laughing.

"Ms. Milholland made us write a letter to ourselves every month the entire year, and, whoa—the drama, the failed romance, the puberty complaints. It was nice to get it all down on paper and let it go," Ms. Lane says. "You're next. You're going to write a letter to yourselves at the beginning of every month for the whole school year. I'll collect the letters, but I won't read them. You have my word. I have enough drama in my life."

Hannah raises her hand. "Where's Greg Johnson now?"

Ms. Lane smiles. "I have no idea. I think that crush only lasted until the next letter. So, you have your homework assignment. Let's move on to poetry. My favorite."

"Ms. Lane, who are they going to get to replace you if you win the election?" Elijah asks. "It's in November, right?"

Ms. Lane is also running for mayor of our town, against a guy named Brent Grimley, who has been the mayor my entire life—and, according to my parents, has accomplished absolutely nothing.

Ms. Lane laughs. "Yes, Election Day is always the first Tuesday in November. I appreciate all the interest around my campaign, including the suggestion from another class that we turn my classroom into my campaign headquarters, but I'm making a firm rule: no discussing the campaign in school. I don't think it's appropriate."

She writes *No Election Talk!* in cursive on a giant hot-pink Post-it and sticks it to the board.

"They're going to get Mr. Linkler, the sub, aren't they?" Elijah says.

"Okay, last thing I'll say is that *if* I were to win, it's a part-time job. So I'll still be your devoted teacher."

"Oh, wow. Mayor is definitely not part-time in Hartford," Shawn says.

"That's because they have a lot of crime in Hartford," Ben says.

"Okay, Ben," Shawn says. "That's why."

"Well, isn't that why the Hartford kids want to go to school here?" Ben asks.

Shawn is one of the Hartford kids.

"You know better than to say something like that, Ben," Ms. Lane says.

"Like what?" Ben says.

"Let's move on," Ms. Lane says, shaking her head.

THE HARTFORD KIDS

I don't know much about the Hartford kids, other than that they live in Hartford, which is a city, like, twenty minutes away from Honey Hill. Their parents had the choice to send them to Hartford schools or bus them to schools in the suburbs, and they chose the suburbs. The Hartford kids pretty much hang out with each other, and eat lunch together, probably because they all ride the same bus to Hartford. Honey Hill is a very white town, so my parents always say, "It's nice we have a program that brings some people of color to the schools. We're big supporters of diversity."

With Lucy home sick, I don't even try to figure out who to sit with in the cafeteria. I go straight to the library.

"Hey, Murphy. How's the day going?" Mr. Beam, the librarian, says with his mouth full of cookie.

"Good."

Mr. Beam and I made an arrangement back in June when Lucy started missing school and I started eating in the library: thirty seconds of small talk, then I do homework and Mr. Beam scrolls through Twitter.

"Tell me one good thing and one lousy thing about your summer," Mr. Beam says.

"Um. The good thing is that my sister, Sarah, had a baby named Penelope, and they're coming here this weekend to get Penelope baptized, and I can't wait to see her. I only saw her when she was a few hours old, and she was sleeping the whole time."

"Congratulations. That's wonderful news."

"And the bad thing is that Lucy is still sick, obviously."

He gives me a pity look. "I'm sorry to hear that. I'll keep her in my thoughts."

"Thanks, Mr. Beam. What about you?"

"Well, let's see. The good thing is that I got to spend a couple weeks at the lake. The bad thing is that it poured the whole time. But it wasn't that bad, because I read a ton of books."

"I should read books," I say. "I pretty much stopped reading in sixth grade."

"I'll get you reading, Murphy. You just need to find the right book."

I take out my yogurt and spoon, open my English binder, and try to figure out how to write a letter to myself.

"We still doing the thirty-second small-talk rule?" Mr. Beam says.

"Yeah. I think that makes sense."

FIRST LETTER TO MYSELF

Dear Mary Kate,

I don't have to give you a lot of background because I am you. Unlike Ms. Lane, I don't have a crush on anyone, so this letter is going to be very boring.

I'm just going to say it. I'm lost without Lucy. I know some people like having big groups of friends or a few friends, but I'm a best-friend person. Being at school without Lucy is like being at a party without shoes or being at a dinner without food. It's depressing and uncomfortable.

Also, Ms. Lane mentioned talking about puberty. Well, I haven't had my period since the first time I got it in July. It's been almost two months, and nothing. Molly got hers right after school ended, and now she gets it every twenty-seven days. She keeps track on an app. I'm constantly checking to see if it's there, and then it's always a false alarm. I don't feel like telling Mom because she's so awkward, so I'm going to ask Sarah about it when she gets here this weekend.

I miss talking to Lucy about literally everything. I've never felt so alone.

Mr. Beam is a very loud chewer. I have to do math homework.

> *Sincerely,*
> *Me*

It's pretty obvious science isn't going to be like the other classes.

I walk in, and Mr. Lu is slumped over his swivel chair, wearing a gas mask, while Rabia stands in front of the smartboard, which has *Words Associated with Climate Change* written across the top.

I sit down, confused.

"Mr. Lu asked me to write your words," Rabia says. "Can somebody please say some words?"

Shawn says, "Burning fossil fuels," and then everyone starts calling out words while Mr. Lu pretends to be dead.

"Nightmares."

"CO_2."

"Methane gas."

"Polar ice caps melting."

"Polar bears starving."

"Total destruction of life."

"Wildfires."

"Really extreme storms."

"Droughts."

"The Climate March."

"Adults ruining everything."

"Deforestation."

"We're all gonna die."

There's nervous laughing after that last one.

Mr. Lu jumps up and yanks off the gas mask. "Okay, okay. That's enough, you doomsday scrollers." He flings the gas mask out the open window. "If we're all going to die, why am I teaching this class? Why am I getting my doctoral degree in environmental education? Why are we bothering to be here? Why?"

Rabia stands awkwardly in front of the class while the rest of us stare at Mr. Lu.

"You can sit, Rabia. Now all of you need to take a moment to breathe. Take in the smell of a hundred half-eaten meatball subs wafting from the cafeteria, and various other middle school odors: armpits, food-stuck-in-braces breath, you know the smells."

A couple people laugh.

"Now, let's regroup. I get it. Climate change is terrifying. In fact, I'm going to call it what it is: a climate crisis. Anyone with a kindergarten science background can see our planet is warming because of our addiction to extracting, processing, and burning fossil fuels so we can have those coveted sneakers you're all wearing and take long showers while listening to bad music."

I look down at everyone's shoes.

"But we're going to start this class on the other side. We're going to build a vision of what a post-addiction planet would look like."

He erases all the words Rabia wrote.

"Close your eyes."

We don't, because it's always awkward when teachers ask us to close our eyes.

"Come on, you're not in seventh grade anymore. Trust the process and close those eyes."

I close my eyes.

"Good. Now picture a planet where we are living in harmony with plants and animals and insects and each other. Touch it. Smell it. Watch it unfold around you. Listen to the sounds of life springing up from places you never expected, of life blooming everywhere."

It's hard to think of anything with Elijah's allergy sniffling next to me.

"Okay, now open your eyes," Mr. Lu says after what seems like an eternity. "Come on. Follow me."

He crawls out the window. Thankfully, his classroom is on the first floor.

We look at one another.

"He said to follow him," Hannah says.

"Do we bring our stuff?" Ben asks.

I shrug.

We roll ourselves out the window and land on the grass.

"Go," Mr. Lu says, shooing us. "Go commune with nature. Get to know all your flora and fauna friends." He points toward the late-summer wildflowers, and the sluggish bees sipping nectar from cardinal flowers, and the woods that connect our neighborhood to the preserve. "We can't save the planet if we don't understand the planet. Come back tomorrow with a written vision of what you want this planet to look like, your version of a perfect world. We'll start there."

People are wandering around aimlessly. I walk over to my favorite birch tree right near the path through the woods to Molly's house. I scrape the rough bark with my finger.

"What kind of tree is that?" somebody says over my shoulder. I turn around and see Shawn squinting up at my tree.

"Birch," I say. "Look how it's bending to try to get better sun."

"It's so cool," he says. "I think this is the kind of tree people used to make canoes."

"I think you're right."

Awkward silence.

"See you later," he says, walking away. "Bye, tree."

"See you later," I say.

I thought I was the only one who talked to trees.

CLIMATE CLASS APPLICATION ESSAY

SHAWN HILL

I am writing to apply to the climate class. My parents were part of a group of citizens in Hartford who fought to get rid of the garbage incinerator that was polluting our city. I want to find other ways to fight polluters who take advantage of communities like ours. It's good news that the incinerator will finally get shut down, but nobody has a good plan for how to deal with the waste that it used to burn, so it's going to be shipped to some other state. I want to work on trying to get people to reduce waste by composting.

My dad is a firefighter who trains people to fight wildfires, which are worsening because of climate change. Wildfires in places like California damage huge sections of land and kill millions of animals—billions if you also count insects, which you should, because insects are very important. I am proud of my dad for being brave, but I am afraid all the time that he might not come home. I have a lot of reasons I want to study climate change, but that's the most important.

I also volunteer at a greenhouse in my neighborhood three days a week, and I deliver the food we grow to families. I know a lot about plants, and I would like to know more about how plants store carbon.

I hope you will consider me for this class.

ALL I KNOW ABOUT THE PEOPLE IN CLIMATE CLASS

- **Jay Mendes:** Has been sitting near me since kindergarten (because Mendes and Murphy are bound together for school eternity). Soccer player.
- **Elijah Campbell:** His parents are from Jamaica and brought in Jamaican food on International Day in third grade. Oldest kid in our class. (I know this because I'm the youngest kid in our class.)
- **Shawn Hill:** Hartford kid. Carries binoculars around (or at least he did in sixth grade).
- **Ben Lettle:** Always talks about Boy Scouts.
- **Rabia Mohammed:** Sometimes sits between Jay and me (*M* names). Visits her grandparents every year in Kashmir and comes back with jet lag. Taught me what jet lag was in first grade.
- **Rebecca Phelps:** Smuggled her cat to school in second grade and let us sneak into the coat room to pet him. Vegetarian, like I am.
- **Hannah Small:** Has a pet rock named Jacqueline. Last year, this bully kid named Nick hid Jacqueline somewhere among all the rocks in the Kindness

Garden. I heard Nick spent the entire summer at a wilderness program for pet-rock throwers and other impossible people.

- **Lucy Perlman:** What *don't* I know about Lucy Perlman? I even know why she went to a urologist today.

THE HAMMOCK

I'm already in the back garden when the bell rings, so I cut through the woods, Will's yard, and Molly's yard, and walk up the street toward my driveway. I keep going onto the path that leads through the preserve and let myself in the back door of Lucy's house.

Her brother, Blake, is yelling at a video game in the basement.

I'm sweating, so I run some water on my wrists, a trick my brother, Mark, taught me a long time ago. I grab two cookies from the panda-bear cookie jar and go out to the hammock on the side of the house, where Lucy's watching bat videos on her phone. I set the cookie on Lucy's forehead.

"Hey," she says. "You can eat it. Not hungry."

Her face is thin and pale.

I hand her the classwork packets I collected from all her teachers. "The only homework is math, write a letter to yourself for English, and write your vision for the planet for climate class. I'll explain it later. I'm tired."

I lie next to Lucy and stare up at the oak tree I've known since I was little.

"How was the 'ologist?" I ask.

"Useless," she says.

"Do you want to talk?"

"Not really. My head is killing me. It's too hot." She's doing the blinking thing again.

"Do you think you'll be able to go to Penelope's christening?"

"I don't know. Can you stop asking me so many questions? I can't deal right now."

"Yeah, I can, Luce."

I'm used to her snapping at me these days.

"I'm going to go now," I say. "I'll see you later."

"'Kay. Bye." She rolls over and closes her eyes.

I pick up my stuff and walk through the preserve toward home.

BEFORE LUCY GOT SICK

Before Lucy got sick, we were perfectly aligned stars. We were campers pitching tents, even in the rain. We were movie watchers in Lucy's den, and book readers in the hammock, and popcorn poppers. We were recorders—of footprints and animal droppings, and feathers, and tufts of hair stuck to trees (scratching posts for bears). Before she got sick, we were searchers—for arrowheads, for bones, for the secret cave we knew we'd find someday. Before she got sick, we were fairy-house builders. We were fairies. We were best friends.

CLIMATE CLASS APPLICATION ESSAY

LUCY PERLMAN

I was excited to learn that Fisher will be having a climate class next year, because I am very worried about climate change and what it means for our planet.

When I was five, I woke up and found a bat hanging from the ceiling in the corner of my room. I know some people would have been scared, but I was so fascinated I sat and stared at the bat all day before I told my parents. I was lucky my dad listened to me and didn't hurt the bat when he took it outside.

Every report I've ever done has been on bats, so I know a lot about them. There's a really bad fungal disease affecting bats. It's called white-nose syndrome, and it's horrible. Scientists believe the disease is spreading and getting worse because of climate change. Without bats we will have many more mosquitoes, which will also carry worse diseases because of climate change.

I will do whatever it takes to stop climate change from destroying bats and everyone else, but first I need to understand it. That's why I want to take this class.

If you can't accept me, please at least accept my best friend, Mary Kate Murphy. We plan to open an eco-lodge together, so one of us definitely needs to learn everything you're going to teach about climate change. Thank you very much.

THE DIARY WITH THE TINY KEY

I'm up in my room trying to figure out how to tie the back of a scratchy sage-green dress, one of Sarah's hand-me-downs from twenty years ago.

Sarah, her husband, Jason, and baby Penelope got here last night. Penelope is a little sweet pea. She's as adorable and pink and wiggly as any baby mammal I have ever met. I love it when she squeezes my finger with her pudgy hand.

I tried to FaceTime Lucy last night. I asked her if there was anything I could do for her. She told me to stop asking that. I asked her why she was mad at me. She told me to stop thinking everything was about me. I know my questions are getting annoying. But there's no good way to say *My life keeps going on while you're miserable in your bed.*

This is the first family event Lucy has missed since we started being friends. I don't know how I'm going to stand in front of everyone at church and be a godmother without her trying to make me laugh from the pews.

Sarah knocks on the door. She's dressed up, in a light-blue skirt and a flowery top.

"I feel like I'm looking in the mirror at myself at twelve," she says. "Except you're much prettier."

"Aw. Thanks," I say, not believing her one bit.

"I brought you a godmother gift," she says, handing me

a box wrapped in cloth and tied with a purple ribbon.

I open it. It's a diary with a tiny key.

"I couldn't have made it through my teen years without my locked diaries," she says. "Now you can write all your private thoughts. Your crushes, all the juicy stuff."

I smile. I can see why Sarah and Ms. Lane are best friends. I don't have the heart to tell my sister that my private thoughts revolve around how to survive climate change and how not to feel sorry for myself because Lucy is sick and mad and not here.

"Thank you, Sarah. I love it."

"I'm so glad you're Penelope's godmother."

"I have a good nickname for her already."

"Oh yeah?"

"Sweet Pea."

"I love it, Mare. She is a sweet pea, isn't she?" She hugs me and helps me retie the bow on the back of the dress. "Now let's go to church and make Mom a happy grandma."

WHY I'M A TWELVE-YEAR-OLD AUNT

When Mom was forty-eight and Dad was fifty-two, Mom thought she was going through menopause. That's when your period stops forever and you can no longer have babies. But it turns out she wasn't in menopause. Her period stopped because she was pregnant with me. My sister and brother were already in college. She and my dad had just opened the bookstore. And out comes baby Mary Kate.

Mom yells at Sarah and Mark when they say I was an oops baby. But I honestly don't mind it. I'm sure I'm not the only oops in the world with parents who look like grandparents and sometimes act like great-grandparents.

THINGS ABOUT HAVING OLDER PARENTS

1. They don't realize everyone else's parents are afraid of things that they wouldn't think about, like cyber creepers and murder hornets, especially since they refuse to own a TV, so they let you run around outside as much as you want.
2. They say things like "Watch your step" and "Well, I'll be a monkey's uncle."
3. They complain about their backs hurting.
4. They get nervous about driving at night.
5. They pretty much live by the saying "Early to bed, early to rise, makes a man healthy, wealthy, and wise." I once asked Dad, "What about women? Do they get to be healthy, wealthy, and wise?" He answered, "Okay, okay, Mary Kate." (I was looking for a real answer.)
6. You can say one minor not-even-bad word, and they'll hear you from any room of the house and yell, "Watch your language." Other than that, they claim they can't hear you.

LETTER TO MY BABY NIECE
ON HER CHRISTENING DAY

Dear Sweet Pea,

Your mom gave me this diary today as a gift for being your godmother. The violets on the cover remind me of spring. The roses remind me of summer. And the pink butterfly sitting on the fattest rose reminds me of you. I've decided to write down everything you'll ever need to know. I plan to give it to you when you're twelve, like I am now. The diary has a lock and a tiny key, so I can tell you all the good stuff.

You had your christening today. When your parents asked me to be your godmother, I didn't really know what that meant. Your grandma said it meant I would hold you in your white gown (the same one your mom and I wore) while Father Milt doused your forehead with holy water. That didn't seem like a huge job. But then your mom said it also meant that I'd be your spiritual guide, and teach you about life, and look out for you when she and your dad can't, and babysit once in a while when they need a break.

I tried to explain to Sarah that Lucy and I are more pagans than Jewish (Lucy) and Catholic (me), but she didn't care about that part. She said she trusts me to guide you. So, I got the job. It makes sense, because your mom has been my everything guide, that's for sure.

Your christening was pretty short. You cried so hard your face turned purple and I was afraid you were going to burst a blood vessel. I could see your tonsils. But I kept holding you while Father Milt did the holy water thing. He didn't seem to care that you were crying. Your dad took you outside after so you didn't bother the next baby. That baby slept through everything. His name was Thomas James Pepper, in case you run into him someday.

Your mom's best friend, Auntie Charlotte, was there. I call her Ms. Lane at school because I don't want to get a good grade and have people say it's because I'm family friends with the teacher. Your uncle Mark came from New York City to be your godfather. He didn't do anything but get stressed-out when you cried. I doubt Mark will have kids. He still acts like a kid.

I rocked you to sleep in the rocking chair while everybody was eating in the backyard. Now you're sleeping in the car seat next to me. You must be dreaming, because you're making faces. What do newborns dream about anyway?

I'll keep writing until I've told you everything you need to know to be a successful twelve-year-old. There's a lot.

Love,
Auntie

SIGNS

It's Labor Day, and people are at our house putting together **CHARLOTTE LANE FOR MAYOR** signs. The signs are butter yellow with navy-blue lettering—the Honey Hill High School colors—with a fat honeybee in the top right corner.

"What's with the honeybee?" Jason asks Charlotte. He's wearing Pea in a carrier, which is all wet from her baby slobber.

"The honeybee is the high school's mascot. We're hoping people associate the bees with town spirit."

Molly comes down the driveway with her dog, Tibby. We sit on the lawn and attach signs to the metal thingies that go into people's yards. She texted last night that she had *news*.

"What's the news?" I ask.

"Good morning to you too," she says. "Well, first, we're starting a social-justice club at HHHS. Me, Bea, Megan, Liza, Pearl, Olivia, Navya, pretty much everybody. We're recruiting Will, Chen, Rahul, and those guys. And Tom, of course. We want to work on a mural project first, where we design and paint murals around town with social-justice themes, like they do in interesting places."

"Do you think the mayor will let that happen?"

"Oh, no. He definitely won't. He wouldn't even let

people do a sidewalk-chalk rainbow on Main Street for Pride Month. But Ms. Lane will. We need to get her elected."

"Yep."

"So, do you want to know the news?"

"I thought that was the news."

"It's news, but *the* news is that your favorite neighbor likes a sophomore."

"Mrs. Caldwell likes a sophomore?"

"Ha ha ha. I'm not saying anything else, because I don't want to jinx it."

Charlotte stands up in her lavender dress and claps her hands like she does when she wants the class to settle down. She thanks everyone for being here and starts speaking in her teacher voice.

"As most of you know, I'm Charlotte Lane. My pronouns are she/her, and I'm running for mayor of Honey Hill because it's time we have a mayor who is ready to get creative and build community."

Everyone claps.

"And I'd like to find meaningful ways to celebrate each and every person who contributes positively to our town."

Louder claps.

"How amazing is my BFF?" Sarah says, sitting down on a deck chair to feed Pea. She unsnaps a bra cup, and Jason slides Pea out of the carrier.

"Amazing enough to be our next mayor," Mom says.

Jay Mendes, one of the kids from climate class, walks up with his mom. I show him how to attach the signs to the metal thingies, and we start talking about the class. I tell him I can't stop thinking about a documentary I watched about how much food is wasted in our country and how disturbing it is, because so many people don't have enough food to eat.

"That's really messed up," Jay says.

Jay's mom comes over and tells him to start loading the car with signs for delivery.

"See you tomorrow."

"Yeah. See you tomorrow."

CLIMATE CLASS APPLICATION ESSAY

JAY MENDES

I would like to attend the climate class next year because my mom says my grandmother is a "climate refugee" and that there are going to be millions more if we all don't do something about climate change.

My grandma was living in a nice house in the country in Puerto Rico when Hurricane Maria hit. She had been through hurricanes in the Caribbean her whole life, but she said this one was different. My grandma and her sister, my great-aunt Carmen, were stuck in their house without power for weeks. The bridge over the river was washed out, and nobody could get to them to give them food or my grandma's diabetes medicine. My dad flew down when the airport finally opened, and he and my uncles had to cross the river to get my grandma and aunt out. My grandma is still upset that they never found her dog, Berti.

My grandma and aunt live with us in Connecticut now, but they miss their home every day. I don't want to see Puerto Rico covered by the ocean. We need to stop climate change from getting worse and worse.

Now that my uncles are getting back on their feet in Puerto Rico, they're farming hemp crops. Hemp is a very strong, fast-growing plant that can be used for food, milk, clothing, a building material called hempcrete, and a lot more. When I was reading about hemp, I found out it's a carbon sink, which means it can absorb a LOT of carbon dioxide, and it even helps keep soil healthy. I am thinking about going back down to Puerto Rico to learn about hemp farming, and I want to know everything I can about how hemp might help with climate change.

THIRD PERIOD

Ms. Lane collects our letters to ourselves, puts them in a big envelope, writes *Period 3* on it in black Sharpie, and puts it in a cabinet. I'm a little nervous. There's no lock on that cabinet. What if somebody grabs the letters and runs? What if *I* grab the letters and run? I would love to know what these people are writing to themselves.

Lucy's mom gave me hers at the christening barbecue. I pull it out of the folder and look down at the paper. I know I shouldn't read it, but once you know how to read, it's impossible to *not* read.

It's more of a list than a letter.

Dear Lucy,
  So tired
  Body hurts everywhere
  Weird feeling in my ears
  Stomach hurts when I eat
  Really bad headaches
  Nausea every night
  Rash
  Bruises on body

Leg and tongue burn
Blurry vision
Sadness
Other bad stuff

Sincerely,
Lucy

AT LUNCH

Mr. Beam is helping a seventh grader find a book about Ida B. Wells. I don't feel like eating. I keep thinking about Lucy's letter. All this time, I've been focused on how miserable I am without her. I should have been thinking about how to help my best friend get better.

I need to text her.

> **ME:** I read the letter.

> **LUCY:** I had to do it for the doctor's appointment. Two birds with one stone, haha.

> **ME:** I'm sorry I never know what to say. And I'm sorry you're going through this.

> **LUCY:** I don't want to die.

My throat fills up with fear.

> **ME:** You're going to be okay, Luce.

She doesn't answer.

EIGHTH PERIOD

We spend the period cutting out pictures from science and nature magazines to cover the bulletin board in the back of Mr. Lu's classroom to go along with our written vision for the planet.

We find fields and flowers and oceans and deserts and penguins and waterfalls and futuristic cars and renewable energy sources, like wind turbines and a giant sun. There are tiny houses with climbing vegetable gardens, and farmers markets, and people hanging out in wild parks. In the middle is the paragraph we wrote as a class, using all of our ideas.

"Whoa," Mr. Lu says, acting like he's going to faint. "You people are more brilliant than all the stars in the universe combined."

He reads our vision very dramatically. " 'The earth is in balance. Ecosystems play like music, each note complementing the next. Humans live in harmony, respecting the role of every living thing. Energy comes from the sun, the wind, the water, the magma beneath us. Food comes from the earth and goes back to the earth. We're not a pyramid with humans at the top. We're a beautiful, complicated, and fully connected symphony.' " Mr. Lu looks like he's going to cry. "Now, isn't this a lot better than that dooms-day stuff you were spewing out like a polluter's chimney the other day?"

We nod.

"I want you to know, though, that this classroom is a safe space for sadness and anger and frustration, and all those other feelings we all have about this crisis. Yes, we're going to focus on the vision, but I won't try to make you feel like your emotions aren't valid. Okay?"

We nod again.

"And here's the most important thing. You are not responsible for what greedy, powerful people have done to this planet. You're thirteen."

"I'm twelve," I say.

"Me too," Ben says.

"Twelve and thirteen," Mr. Lu says. "The first rule of climate club is: 'We can all activate our superpowers to heal the earth.' But kids are not the problem. Polluters and the governments that prop them up are the problem. Get it?"

Silence.

"Get it?"

"Yes," we say.

"Now we're a climate club?" Rebecca says.

"No. It's a play on words from an old movie. Anyway, I think 'club' sounds cooler than 'class.' Whatever. Focus on the rule."

"What movie?" Elijah says.

"You're missing the point. Repeat after me: We all have superpowers."

We say it.

"Louder."

"We all have superpowers."

"And so we begin. Let's put on those capes and get to work," Mr. Lu says. "For our first project of the year, we're going to start with our own neighborhood. We'll come up with some pieces of the solution pie that we care about, and then find ways to create community projects around those solutions."

"I really want to do something about fast fashion and how it contributes to climate change," Hannah says.

"Yes. Done. You are on it. What else? Shout it out. I know you've been waiting for this moment."

"Leaf blowers," Ben shouts. "I want to make leaf blowers illegal!"

"Oh yeah, that's bold. Ben's got his topic."

"People need to go vegetarian," Rebecca says. "I seriously don't even know if I can be friends with meat-eaters anymore. They disgust me."

"I eat meat," Elijah says.

"Me too," Jay says.

"Okay, we're going to talk about *how* to deliver messages later, Rebecca," Mr. Lu says. "I don't necessarily think telling people they're disgusting is going to win them over. But is it safe to say your topic is meat consumption and climate change?"

"Uh, yeah. Obviously."

I look down at my desk and try to think of something. I'm lost. I feel like maybe I shouldn't be in this class. Everyone else already knows what they want to do.

Jay chooses hemp farming.

Shawn chooses composting.

Rabia chooses electric vehicles, and then Elijah says electric vehicles was his idea too, so Mr. Lu says, "The more the merrier," and puts them together.

"There are a *lot* of people energizing this classroom right now, and I'm here for it," Mr. Lu says. "Okay, Murphy. What've you got?"

"I'm not sure, exactly. I've been thinking about this documentary I watched about how much food is wasted in our country and how food waste contributes to climate change."

"That's perfectly aligned with Shawn's topic. How about you two pair up?"

I'm not even sure I want to do food waste. It's the only thing I could think of. But Shawn is already moving his chair over to my desk.

"Can you give an example of a project?" Hannah asks Mr. Lu.

"I'm leaving this open so you can be creative, but maybe a bulletin-board display at all the schools in town, or at the post office, even. Maybe you can perform skits for the younger kids, or design a pamphlet. I'm counting on you to think outside the box."

"We should go bigger," Shawn says.

"Like, what do you mean?" Mr. Lu says.

"I think we should go bigger than a skit or a bulletin board."

"Now you're talking," Mr. Lu says. "Go big or go home." The bell rings. "Well, for now, just go home."

CLIMATE CLASS APPLICATION ESSAY

ELIJAH CAMPBELL

I am applying to join the new climate class next year because I am interested in electric vehicles. I might even want to be an EV engineer, but I would like to know more about it and if EVs are the best thing for the environment or if there's something even better that we don't know about yet.

Right now, I know that transportation is one of the biggest causes of climate change. The exhaust from cars, buses, planes, and other vehicles travels up to the atmosphere and sits there warming the earth. Electric vehicles don't burn gas, but they use electricity to charge their batteries, which means an EV won't be completely emission-free unless the power source it's plugging into uses clean energy, like solar or wind. I would like to learn how we can quickly transition our grid to clean energy.

Also, I don't think people understand how bad car idling is for the climate. I always see people sitting in their cars in parking lots on their phones, with engines running. It's a huge pet peeve of mine.

I'm very interested in doing whatever I can to help our environment, and I hope you will accept me for the class. I have spent a lot of time talking about this with my science teacher, Mr. Phipps, and he said I can use him as a reference.

LOVELY PEOPLE

Mom comes home from the bookstore early on Tuesdays and Thursdays. "To help you with your schoolwork," she says—which I haven't needed since the fourth grade. She cleans the first floor on Tuesdays and the second floor on Thursdays, except for the bathrooms, which is, unfortunately, my job. She eats crackers with cream cheese, reads the gardening section of the newspaper, and usually goes out to weed until it's time to make dinner.

Mom speaks louder than most human beings when she's on the phone. I'm in my room, trying to FaceTime Lucy for the seventh time since I got home from school, when I hear Mom shouting on the phone with Lucy's mom.

"Oh, I'm so sorry to hear that."

"Did anything set her off? What reason does she have to be so angry?"

"Okay, I'll let her know."

"Yes. Stay in touch. Let me know if you need anything."

She stomps up the stairs in her gardening boots, knocks twice, and flings open my door.

"Hi, Mary Kate. How was school?"

"What's wrong with Lucy?"

She looks surprised for a second. "She's in a rage, and she threw a salad spinner at her mom. Thank goodness it was just the plastic basket part and nobody got hurt. I can't for the life of me figure out why she's so angry. Her parents are lovely people."

"Mom, there's something very wrong with her. She's not angry for no reason. She's sick. It's making her act like that. Why doesn't anyone get this?"

"Mary Kate, she's been seeing a whole lot of doctors. Anyway, her mom said she's resting now, so don't try to call her, because she wants her to get good sleep."

"Fine."

"Are you upset with me?"

"No, Mom. I'm frustrated that nobody is helping my friend."

"That's not fair."

"Well, is she any better?"

"They're trying their best."

"I have to do my homework."

"Sounds good." She closes the door.

I turn on my laptop and watch a video Mr. Lu assigned about fossil fuels. It's exactly the kind of thing Lucy would love.

FACETIME WITH SHAWN HILL

SHAWN: Hey.

ME: Hey. Do you have any ideas for the project?

SHAWN: I mean, I do, but do you want to go first?

ME: I don't have any ideas yet.

SHAWN: I volunteer at a greenhouse in my neighborhood, and we do a lot of composting.

ME: Wait, don't you live in Hartford?

SHAWN: Yeah, believe it or not, there are green things in Hartford.

ME: Oh, sorry.

SHAWN: What if we try to get a composting program going at school? Have you seen how much food kids throw out in our cafeteria?

ME: I love that idea. I don't even know why they bother serving lunch at that place. And Lucy will probably want to join our group when she gets back.

SHAWN: Where is Lucy, anyway?

ME: She's sick. Nobody knows what's wrong with her. She has all these bizarre symptoms. It's really stressful.

SHAWN: My dad had something like that, and my mom found this doctor down near New York who finally figured out what was wrong with him. Do you want me to get the guy's name?

ME: Let me ask Lucy. Actually, yes, get his name.

SHAWN: Okay, I will.

ME: Are you free to meet after school tomorrow to work on the project?

SHAWN: I have to work. Can you come to the greenhouse where I volunteer?

ME: Yes. I'll be there.

TEXTS WITH LUCY

LUCY: I'm better today. Yesterday
was so bad. I felt like my entire
brain was on fire.

ME: That's horrible. I'm so sorry,
Luce.

LUCY: Thank you for checking
on me. I feel like nobody else at
school even remembers me.

ME: Everyone is asking about you.

That's a lie. Other than Molly, Shawn, and a couple
people from the basketball team, nobody has bothered to
ask about Lucy.

LUCY: That's nice.

ME: I had to FaceTime Shawn Hill
about our science project. His dad
was really sick, and they found a

> doctor near New York who helped
> him get better. Do you want the
> doctor's name?

I assume she's going to ignore me or get annoyed, but she texts back right away.

LUCY: Yes.

FLYER ON THE WALL

Dad wakes up every morning at five thirty. He walks our German shepherd, Murphy (yes, our dog's name is Murphy Murphy), and our beagle, Claudia, then he picks up the paper from the end of the driveway, makes yogurt with granola in the spring and summer, or oatmeal with raisins and maple syrup in the fall and winter, and sits at the kitchen table with his glasses on, reading the paper, eating his yogurt or oatmeal, and grumbling about news stories.

Today, even though it's eighty degrees at 7:00 a.m. again, he's eating oatmeal, because every year he switches from yogurt to oatmeal the day after Labor Day.

"Hey, Mare, check this out." He pulls a flyer from under the pile of newspapers. "Somebody from the town hung this on the bulletin board at the bookstore yesterday. I'm thinking maybe you can give it to Molly and the dress-code crew. We need to get some new blood coming up with ideas. Otherwise, somebody will propose another bank or liquor store and call it a community project."

Dad has many opinions. One is that he doesn't agree with pretty much anything our mayor says or does. And another is that he doesn't think our town needs another bank or liquor store. I look at the flyer.

COMMUNITY GRANT OPPORTUNITY

Mayor Grimley has announced the first annual **APPLEFEST COMMUNITY GRANT AWARD**. Residents of Honey Hill can showcase a project idea for improving the town.

Community members will vote for their favorite proposal on *September 25th from 10:00 a.m. to 5:00 p.m. at APPLEFEST*.

The winner will receive $10,000 to complete the project.

Apply at Town Hall by September 21st.

"Seems like a gimmick to win votes for himself," Dad says. "Typical for that stuffed shirt."

"Can I take this?" I ask.

"That's why I brought it home, my dear."

DEFINITION

stuffed shirt *(noun)*

a smug, conceited person, with a pompous, conservative attitude

Synonyms: fuddy-duddy, stick-in-the-mud, dud, tool

ON THE BUS

I show Molly the Applefest grant flyer. She takes a picture of it and texts it to our friend Pearl.

"This would be perfect for our mural project," she says. "It would pay for all the supplies, everything."

"Your club should definitely apply," I say.

I keep the flyer, just in case I get ideas of my own.

AT LUNCH

Shawn convinces me to sit with him and his friends at lunch so we can take notes on how much food people throw out to build our case for school composting.

I feel like I'm abandoning Mr. Beam.

I look around. They're serving tuna fish on a roll, salad, and apples. I swear 90 percent of the trays are full when kids dump them in the big green trash cans. This is probably because we can also buy ice cream cups and bags of chips, which are the only things people actually eat.

I take out my notebook and try to keep track of the number of trays that are nearly full when they're dumped. It's too many to count.

"I never noticed it was this bad," I say.

"I ate everything on my tray," Shawn's friend Gabe says.

"Yeah, because I dared you to," Shawn says.

"The tuna fish tasted like foot," Gabe says. "Maybe we should make decent food a school project, and then they wouldn't waste everything."

"I doubt it," I say.

Shawn and I decide to go up to the woman with the SUE name tag who is standing at the register.

"Hi. I'm Shawn Hill, and this is Mary Kate Murphy. We're doing a project in science class, and we're wondering if we could talk to you about getting a composting program started at Fisher Middle School."

Sue stares at us blankly for a second and then says, "That's something my boss tried to do a couple years ago, but nobody was interested. Talk to the superintendent. They make those kinds of decisions."

"Thank you," we say.

"I'd love to see composting here," Sue says. "I compost everything at home. We have a big compost heap and a vegetable garden."

Sue is with us. That can't hurt.

I take pictures of the tuna-roll graveyard that's piled up in the trash cans. It's gross, and I can't believe I've lived this long without noticing how disturbing it is.

Mr. Lu comes running in, all sweaty and out of breath.

"Sorry, I got caught up in a conversation about TV shows with the gym teachers." He looks around. "Wow. You're already working. I might as well go back to the gym and watch some shows on Mr. Castle's laptop."

I raise my hand.

"Yes, Mary Kate? Do you have a show suggestion?"

"No, my parents are weird, and we don't have a TV. Don't ask." I unfold the flyer. "There's a grant competition at Applefest this year. They're giving out ten thousand dollars to the best community project. They're letting people vote on project ideas at Applefest, and the winner gets the money."

Mr. Lu smacks the desk, and we all jump. "This!" he says, grabbing the flyer from my hand. "This is epic. Way to connect the dots, Murphy. Hill, you wanted to go bigger? Here's your chance. We're going to get some Benjamin Franklins for climate class."

Mr. Lu does a bizarre dance.

"Let's brainstorm how we can take our project seedlings and grow them into a community proposal," he says. "Put your ideas together this week, and we'll discuss Friday."

"Wait, what? We only have until Friday to get this done?" Hannah says.

"The first rule of climate club is: 'Learn how to work under pressure.' Time is not on our side, but I think it's worth a shot."

"I thought the first rule of climate club was about our superpowers," Elijah says.

"You're missing the point. Come up with a couple sentences, and we'll go from there."

We sit around trying to think quickly until the bell rings.

"You still coming to the greenhouse?" Shawn says.

"Yes," I say. "I'll be there."

THE GREENHOUSE

I walk to the bookstore after school and order lavender tea from Ayana at the coffee bar while Mom helps a customer find romance novels in large print.

"Will you take me to see the kid I'm doing my project with?" I ask Mom.

"Okay, give me a minute. Can you put the address in my GPS thing?"

I wait in the car for what seems like a year.

"This says 'Hartford,'" Mom says when she's finally ready to go.

"Yes. He lives in Hartford."

"Oh, come on. You didn't tell me that, Mary Kate. I thought I was driving someplace local. I have to get back to the store."

"Mom, I have to do this proposal. Can you please drop me off and have Dad get me later?"

She shakes her head and taps the steering wheel all the way to Hartford. When we get past the red light near the bakery Dad likes, she looks at me and says, "Mary Kate, this is not a good neighborhood. Couldn't you have had him to our house?"

"There's nothing wrong with this neighborhood, Mom. And he has a volunteer job. I don't have any job."

"I have no idea where I'm going to park."

"You're not parking. You're dropping me off."

"I don't feel comfortable dropping you off and leaving."

She locks the doors.

"Are you seriously locking the doors? Because that seems like a really racist thing to do. All I see are people minding their own business."

She slams on the brakes as a guy carrying a bag of groceries crosses the street in front of her. "Don't you dare accuse me of being racist."

"You just locked your doors because you saw Black people walking around."

"I can't believe you're saying this to me right now."

"Pull over. That's the greenhouse across the street."

I feel awful that my mom is being so out of control, and there's Shawn standing in front of the greenhouse with a garden hoe and a big plastic container.

She pulls over in front of a fire hydrant, and I jump out.

"I'll text Dad when I'm done." I close the door and wave.

Her face is all red. She freezes in the middle of the road until somebody honks at her and she drives away.

"Hey. Do you still carry around binoculars?" Shawn asks when I get across the street.

I laugh. "Sometimes. You never know when you're going to see something good. Do you?"

"No, I stopped when I got to middle school. But I'm considering getting them out again."

"Highly recommend." I'm trying to act normal, but my heart is beating hard from that conversation with Mom.

"I have never seen an actual bear," he says.

"You didn't see the one that was looking in the window of Ms. Santos-Skinner's office last year? When they called a Code Brown?"

"No. That was the one day I was at the orthodontist."

"I'll take you to the preserve sometime. They're all over the place."

We go into the greenhouse. It's hot and muggy and full of all kinds of plants. Shawn introduces me to Shirley, the lady who brought the greenhouse to the neighborhood. She's very excited to show me her strawberries.

Yeah, terrible neighborhood, Mom.

Shirley leaves, and I help Shawn water the plants. He points out a big pile of compost. "This soil is amazing. It's so much better than the stuff you get at the store."

Then we sit at a table in an office connected to the greenhouse and pull out our notes.

"Before I forget, Lucy definitely wants that doctor's name."

"Okay. I'll ask my mom. I feel bad for Lucy. We were really worried about my dad for a while."

"But he's okay now?"

"He's fine. It was a weird viral infection. He's actually in California. He trains people on forest fire mitigation."

"What's that, exactly?"

"He works on stopping gigantic wildfires before they spread."

"That's awesome."

"It is, but he's been gone since July. We all really miss him."

Dad texts me: **Your mother is worried. You okay?**

I text Sarah in Boston: **Mom dropped me in Hartford and**

is worried because she's being racist and thinks I'm going to get murdered or something. I'm trying to do a school project. Can you deal with this?

Sarah texts back right away: **Ughhh. Yes.**

I feel bad texting this while Shawn is sitting here emailing a composting company about how much it would cost to compost at our middle school.

"So once we find out how much it will cost," I say, "then we'll ask the superintendent if we can afford to do it, right?"

"Yes, and if not, maybe we can try to get the ten-thousand-dollar grant to pay for it."

"Good plan. I think we're done," I say. "What made you so interested in composting?"

"Do you know about the incinerator?"

"No."

"It's been burning trash from all over Connecticut and polluting Hartford for a long time. My parents are part of an environmental group that fought to get rid of it because it's causing asthma in kids and a ton of other health problems. It's like one big racist mess."

"How is an incinerator racist?"

He raises his eyebrows and asks, "Do you have an incinerator in Honey Hill?"

"No."

"Where do you think your Honey Hill trash goes?"

"I don't know."

"It goes to our incinerator because the fancy people in Honey Hill won't let anybody build an incinerator in their town and pollute their kids' lungs."

"Oh. I get it."

"Anyway, the incinerator is shutting down, but the trash is still a problem. We need to make less trash, and composting is good for a lot of reasons."

"There's much more to all this than I thought," I say.

I help Shawn water lettuce plants until Dad pulls up in front of the greenhouse and meets us out front. He shakes Shawn's hand firmly and says, "Hey, my main man. How's it going?"

"Sorry, my hands are pretty dirty," Shawn says.

"It's all good," Dad says.

I want to die.

In the car, I text my sister: **Dad was trying to talk like a Black guy when he met the kid I'm doing the project with. Help me.**

Sarah texts back: **I'm so sorry! I'll work on them.**

THE DOCTOR AT THE END OF THE ROPE

Shawn messages me after eleven. I'm still up, trying to figure out how to make composting look exciting enough to get us the Applefest money.

> Dr. Denwood Houlish. He's an
> immunologist. My mom says
> he's the best. He doesn't take
> insurance, so it's expensive.

I Google Dr. Denwood Houlish. I've never seen a doctor with so many we-were-at-the-end-of-our-rope-and-he-saved-my-life comments. I send his number and the comments to Lucy. For the first time since she got sick, I feel a tiny bit hopeful.

AT BREAKFAST

Mom acts like nothing happened in the car yesterday. That's her usual thing. She hands me a peanut-butter bar and my water bottle and says, "Have a good day." But her *Have a good day* is flat.

"You too, Mommy," I say in my fake-cheerful voice.

Sarah always says, "Don't bother trying to talk things out with our parents. Just call me."

I've been doing that for twelve years. I don't know if I want to do it anymore.

THE EMAIL WE WRITE
TO THE SUPERINTENDENT

Dear Dr. Eastman,

Our names are Mary Kate Murphy and Shawn Hill. We're students in Mr. Lu's climate class. We have noticed that far too much food is wasted during lunch at Fisher Middle School. You may or may not know that Honey Hill's food waste goes into landfills, and when it decomposes, it releases methane gas, a huge contributor to climate change. We believe that we could make a big difference by composting the food waste at Fisher.

Can you help us start a composting program at Fisher Middle School?

Thank you very much. We are so glad you are our superintendent.

Sincerely,
Mary Kate and Shawn

THE FASTEST EMAIL RESPONSE
IN HUMAN HISTORY

Dear Shawn and Mary Kate,

What a delight to receive your email about composting at Fisher Middle School. I checked in with a couple administrators I know who are doing this in other districts, and they're super happy with their programs.

You probably know how budget stuff works— SLOWLY. I don't want you to have to wait until we get approval to fund this. So here's my thought: if your class can raise the money to pay for composting services for the rest of the school year and show the powers that be how effective the program is, I'll make sure it's fully funded next school year, AND I'll even try to get the program going at every school in the district.

Please reach out anytime. Mr. Lu can give you my cell number if you need to call. I'm excited about the great work you're doing.

> *My very best,*
> *Bernadette Eastman*
> *(Bern)*

WHEN YOUR FAVORITE NEIGHBOR
BECOMES YOUR BIGGEST COMPETITION

There's hardly anyone on the bus. People have scattered to sports, after-school clubs, and the woods near the library, the only place in town parents don't know about.

Molly sprints out the side door of the high school, waving her arms as the bus is about to leave. She takes a minute to gasp for air, then sits in the seat across from me. "Sorry, I'm really sweaty and smelly. I need my own seat."

"Where were you?"

"Our club took a quick vote. We're going to do the mural idea for the Applefest grant thing. Bea and Pearl are coming up with some designs, and we're going to make poster-size mock-ups for the display. I'm getting the application done tonight."

"Okay, don't hate me, but I have to tell you something."

"Uh-oh. What is it?"

"Our climate class is submitting an application for Applefest too."

"Oh, that's it? Why would I hate you? You're the one who gave me the idea. What are you doing?"

"We're still trying to figure that out."

"I'm just glad people will have good choices." She looks down at her phone. "Subject change?"

"Okay?"

She shows me a side-view photo of a kid wearing a blue baseball cap. "I took a picture of the sophomore when he wasn't looking. I made Navya try to convince him to join our social-justice club. He lives on her street."

"He looks good from the side," I say.

When Molly gets off the bus, I stay on and take it to Lucy's stop.

I'm already starting a climate-class group chat: **The high school social-justice club is entering the Applefest grant contest with a really good idea. I hope you're thinking.**

LANGUAGE

When I get to Lucy's, her aunt Michelle's car and my mom's car are in the driveway.

Something is off.

I run up the back steps, and they're sitting at the kitchen table, drinking tea. "What's wrong with Lucy?" I ask.

"Hon, she had to go to the hospital," her aunt Michelle says. The words float through the kitchen in slow motion. "She's struggling with mental health. She needs to be stabilized."

"Something is causing all of this," I say, "and nobody will try to figure it out."

"Mary Kate, she had a breakdown," Mom says. "She tore the house apart and pulled off her clothes. She said she felt like bugs were crawling on her. They need to get her checked out. Maybe it is in her head, like Dad has been saying."

"Wait, Dad has been saying Lucy's symptoms are in her head? What the freak, Mom?"

"Hey. Language."

"*Language?* Are you kidding me? You're sitting here trying to tell me Lucy is faking?"

"No, that's not what your mom is saying," Aunt Michelle

says. "She's saying the origin of her symptoms might be mental-health-related."

I'm in a rage storm right now. I want to break their teacups with my face.

I throw my backpack on the floor and run out the door toward the preserve. I go straight to the place Lucy and I call the panic room, the crumbled stone wall surrounded by cattails at the edge of the pond, where we always meet when we're having a horrible day.

I want so badly for Lucy to be there waiting for me so she can make jokes about my parents being from an old New England almanac, and I can make jokes about her parents being Brooklyn hipsters, and we can pretend the cattails are guys named Tony or Randolf to make each other laugh.

I push the tall grass out of the way and sit on a toppled piece of wall.

I stare at the ripples in the pond and recite over and over again: *Please get better. Please get better. Please get better.*

I don't know how long I've been staring at the woodpecker trying to peck at a twig way too small for her to get anything out of, but then again, why should I judge a woodpecker when I can't even be a good friend?

"Mare Bear?" I hear Molly's voice calling me from the other side of the birch grove. She knows about the panic room. Lucy and I wrote her a long letter when we were nine about how the panic room was only for Lucy and me but that we wanted her to know about it in case of an emergency, and she could visit if she was lonely, but she wasn't allowed to tell her brother, Danny, because he wasn't nice.

"I'm here," I say, waving my hand.

She pushes through the cattails and stops a few feet from me.

"Hey," she says softly. "Your mom sent me."

"I assumed."

"She said you were having a bad day."

"They took Lucy to a mental health hospital," I say. "She freaked out and felt like bugs were crawling all over her."

"Oh no."

"Now my parents and her aunt Michelle are saying it's all in her head." I shut my eyes and open them. "It's not,

Molls. I know Lucy better than anyone. When she had strep throat last year, she was fighting with her mom to let her go to school. She would never stay home for no reason. She was completely fine, and then suddenly she wasn't."

"I wish I could do something. It's, like, such a helpless feeling."

"I'm just glad you're here." I stand up and wipe the dirt off my butt.

We walk through the birch grove and the sunflower field, slapping at the mosquitoes that keep attacking our ankles. Molly hugs me and runs toward her house. I'm almost home when my phone vibrates in my pocket.

It's Lucy.

"Are you okay?" I say, relieved to hear her voice.

"Yeah, I'm okay. But, Mare, I'm having this creepy feeling all over my body. It's like ghost bugs tickling me. And nobody believes me."

"Luce, I believe you, and I'm going to find help for you. Where are you now?"

"I'm at the hospital. I feel really bad for the kids here, Mare."

"Lucy, try to sleep until you can get out of there."

"I have to go. They're taking my phone. Please make them believe me."

She hangs up.

I've never been able to make anyone do anything.

But I have to try.

THIRD PERIOD

We were supposed to analyze poems for homework, and I'm praying Ms. Lane doesn't ask me a question. My hair is greasy, my head hurts, my heart hurts, and I want the day to be over so I can check on Lucy.

"Okay, grab a partner, and let's dive a little deeper into how Langston Hughes and Edna St. Vincent Millay convey a sense of place in their poetry."

Shawn taps me on the arm. I jump.

"You want to be partners?"

"I forgot to do the assignment. I think I should go to the nurse."

"No, come on. I can explain this in five minutes." He squints at me. "Is something wrong? You seem really distracted."

I've noticed Shawn talks like a forty-year-old sometimes. "I'm so worried about Lucy. I don't know what to do."

"Did you give her that doctor's name?"

I can't tell him she's in the hospital because she feels like ghost bugs are crawling on her. "Yes. I'm going to remind her as soon as I can see her."

I stand in a bathroom stall and call Mom. "Do you have any news about Lucy?"

"Yes. She's on her way home. They increased her anxiety medicine and gave them a referral to a good therapist. I bet she'll be on the mend soon."

I feel like there are hornets in my throat. "She won't."

"Why do you have to be so negative, Mary Kate?"

"I'm not being negative. I know lots of kids with anxiety. It's not like this."

"Mary Kate, you're twelve. I understand you're frustrated, and worried about Lucy. We all are. But let the doctors do their thing."

"The doctors are useless." I hang up and walk down to the library.

"You okay?" Mr. Beam asks.

Shawn's at a table in the back, waiting for me to help write our proposal. I nod and take the deepest breath I've ever taken. I exhale all the way to Shawn's table and force myself to focus on composting.

EIGHTH PERIOD

Mr. Lu has now decided he wants us all to have partners for the projects, but Ben refuses to give up the leaf-blower idea and Rebecca refuses to give up the vegetarian idea. Jay and Hannah are going to combine fast fashion and hemp, and Elijah and Rabia are doing electric vehicles, and Shawn and I are doing composting. So that's five groups, and five groups is too many groups to be in the grant competition.

"I have a thought. Hear me out," Mr. Lu says. "Why don't you each put together a budget, including how your project could benefit from ten grand. I mean, if you can do your project for free, that's great. We'll focus on the project that could most benefit from the money."

"How do we decide which project that is?" Rabia asks.

"We do what we do in any democracy. We vote."

"Won't everyone vote for themselves?" Elijah says.

"Ah. You vote for a project that isn't your own, dear sir."

Mr. Lu goes to his laptop and turns on classical music, but a few minutes later, Mr. Dern bangs on the door and tells him to take it down a notch.

Shawn and I crawl out the window so we can call the

composting company because we don't have time to wait around for a response to our email.

"A middle school with four hundred students, depending on how much waste, would be about three hundred fifty dollars a month," the composting-company woman says.

That's about $3,500 for the school year.

THE PROPOSAL PITCHES

- **Elijah and Rabia:** "We would like to teach the community about electric vehicles by having an electric-vehicle car show. We don't really need money to do this if car dealers are willing to bring cars to the school parking lot."
- **Hannah and Jay:** "We want to have a clothing swap where people bring gently used items and swap them for other items. At the clothing swap, we will have information about hemp and hemp clothing. We would need about eight hundred dollars for clothing racks and hangers and to buy some hemp clothing."
- **Ben:** "I want to go door-to-door to tell people how bad leaf blowers are for the environment and offer to rake leaves the old-fashioned way for free. This won't cost money."
- **Rebecca:** "I would like to make a documentary film showing how horrifying it is to murder animals in factory farms and how going meatless will save animals and reduce emissions. It would cost at least ten thousand dollars for film equipment and transportation to get me to factory farms where I will secretly film."

- **Shawn and Mary Kate:** "We want to start a composting pilot program at Fisher Middle School. We will teach everyone about how to reduce food waste and then compost whatever food we do waste. The cost of this will be about three thousand five hundred dollars for composting services for one school year. If we can get the Applefest grant, we could use the extra money to pay for other schools in the district to start composting programs too."

THE WINNER

I don't know if it's because Rebecca's project isn't very realistic and the other projects don't need as much money, but composting wins. Now we actually have to do the project.

SUNFLOWERS

I can't sleep, even though it's Saturday. I walk the dogs and then go straight to Lucy's house. The preserve looks so pretty. The sunflower field glows in the morning sun. I stop and break off a flower for Lucy. It smells like the end of summer.

When I get to the house, I recognize Lucy's grandma's burgundy-colored car next to Aunt Michelle's Volkswagen. Michelle is probably in there stressing everybody out. Like Lucy's dad always says, "Michelle gives her two cents whether we want it or not."

I knock on the screen door. They're all in the kitchen: Lucy's parents, her grandma, Michelle, and Blake, who is patting Priscilla the cat on her head (which she hates).

"Hey, Mary Kate. Come in," Lucy's dad says.

"Maybe now isn't a good time for friend visits," Aunt Michelle says, giving her two cents.

"No, come in, hon. Go on up," her mom says.

Lucy's sitting on the bed scratching her legs.

"Are you okay?" I ask.

"No," she says.

I dump some old, brown, rotting wildflowers into the trash can in Lucy's bathroom and fill the vase with fresh water. I stick in the sunflower and set it on the sunny spot on her windowsill.

There are welts all over Lucy's arms, legs, and stomach. She's gotten so skinny, it's scary.

"I know you're sick of doctors, but I have that doctor's name, and I trust Shawn Hill. He's not going to give the name of somebody useless."

She pulls up the comforter and crawls under the covers.

"I already said yes," she says. "It can't be worse than what I just went through."

"Really?"

"Yes. You just have to figure out how to convince my parents."

I close the curtains, turn off the lights, and lie on the bed next to Lucy until she falls asleep.

When I get up to leave, her mom, her grandma, and Aunt Michelle are in the kitchen, talking about how they're going to cancel Lucy's bat mitzvah.

"Wait, you're canceling the bat mitzvah?" I say.

Lucy's mom puts her finger to her lips.

She whispers, "We have to, hon. She's not going to be ready for a bat mitzvah in a month. She'll be able to do the service when she's better."

"That's too bad," I say. But I know it might not be that bad, because Lucy was dreading the party. Parties aren't Lucy's thing.

I start walking toward the door, and then I stop. I pull a piece of paper with Dr. Houlish's information out of my pocket and unfold it. My hands are clammy.

"My friend's dad had a mysterious sickness, and this doctor helped him get better. I really hope you'll take Lucy to see him." And then the tears I've been holding back burst out of my eye sockets. It's so embarrassing.

Lucy's mom gets up and traps me in hug, and I'm struggling to breathe. "I know this is hard, Mary Kate."

I manage to get out some muffled words. "Will you take her? You can look up the good reviews. He's saved a lot of people."

She takes the paper. "We'll definitely look into it."

"Okay. Thank you."

When I get home, I text Lucy: **I gave your mom the information. She said she'll definitely look into it.**

I know she's sleeping, but I finally feel relief, like things are going to be better soon.

THE BIG TOUR

Shawn's mom drops him off and gets out to introduce herself to Mom and Dad, who are wearing matching floppy hats and planting mums near the mailbox.

Please don't start talking about your Black Lives Matter display at the bookstore, I silently beg my parents.

Shawn climbs out of the back of the car carrying binoculars, his backpack, and a bag full of chili ingredients. He wants to make me the vegetarian chili his dad makes at the fire station.

"You didn't need to bring your own lunch, Shawn," Mom says.

"It's fine, Mom," I say. "We're doing a cooking project thing."

Dad can't resist giving Shawn and his mom and his little sister, Sydney, a tour of our gardens, and they get into a long, boring conversation about squash. Dad runs around looking for a good basket to fill with squash for Shawn's family, and Shawn, his mom, and I stand at the garden fence awkwardly while my mom brings out iced tea and Shawn's sister plays with Murphy and Claudia.

After we finally drink the iced tea, get the basket of squash into their trunk, and shove Murphy out of their car because he wants to go home with Sydney, they leave, and Shawn and I walk straight toward the preserve. It's like we can read each other's minds.

"Is this an actual barn with animals?" Shawn asks as we pass through my backyard.

"No. My dad has his wood workshop in there, and my brother, Mark, set up a band room upstairs. He and his strange friends had a band when he was younger. I'll show you later."

Shawn follows me down the path we call Golden Alley because of all the goldenrod this time of year.

"This is definitely the nicest part of Honey Hill," he says.

"Why did your parents decide to send you to school in Honey Hill, instead of Hartford?" I ask him.

"When I was little, they said it was because we had the same last name as the town, and I actually believed that answer. Get it? Shawn Hill and Honey Hill? Then they said it was because schools here have more resources. That's all I ever hear: resources, resources, resources."

"Do you think that's true?"

"It depends on what you think resources are, but whatever. I don't really get to decide my own school situation. Trust me, I wouldn't choose Honey Hill."

"Really? Why not?"

"It's like I don't belong in this town, and then I go home and my friends there have all these inside jokes, and—I don't know—I just wish things were different."

"But aren't you glad you're getting a good education?"

"If dealing with racist nonsense is a good education, then yeah."

I stop asking questions.

We cut through the woods and reach the top of the sledding hill.

"Do you want the big tour or the mini tour?" I ask.

"I think the big tour."

THINGS I SHOW SHAWN HILL

- The kettle hole that was made by a glacier
- The way the trees in the birch grove all stretch toward the sun
- The pond and the cattails
- The remains of the raft Lucy and I made out of branches and twine
- The popper things and the crunchy things we like to step on
- The sunflowers
- The site of the hornet situation

THINGS I DON'T SHOW SHAWN HILL

- The fairy-house village
- The panic room
- The animal graveyard

Shawn doesn't need to know how strange we are.

THE HORNET SITUATION

When Lucy and I were younger and a little too fearless, we found what we thought was a hornets' nest in a tree near the pond. We watched the hornets go in and out until it was night and the nest was quiet. Then we took one of those long skewers for s'mores and decided it would be fun to poke the nest. The hornets woke up, flew out, stung me, stung Lucy, stinging us again and again, and we ended up in the pond with only our eyes and noses sticking out, like alligators.

We ran to Lucy's house and covered ourselves with pink calamine lotion and never told our parents. We didn't want them to tell us we were too young and fearless to go to the preserve alone anymore.

We found out later they weren't even hornets—they were a different species of wasp—but we still call it the hornet situation, and that's what it will always be.

Shawn uses his binoculars to look at the hawks' nest at the top of the creepiest dead tree. We find a bare spot on a tree near the pond with tufts of coarse black hair around the edges.

"Bear scratching post," I say.

"Can we wait a while?" he asks.

"They never come when you're waiting for them," I say. "I bet you'll see them next time."

When we get to the house, Mom and Dad are eating sandwiches and pickles on the screened porch. I've never seen them eat a sandwich without a pickle.

Shawn and I take out all the ingredients for the vegetarian chili, and Shawn shows me how to chop the onion into tiny pieces. We put the beans, the onion, the tomatoes, and the spices in a big pot and let it bubble.

"Smells divine," Mom says.

"It's my dad's special recipe," Shawn says. "The secret ingredient is brown sugar."

We bring bowls of chili up to my brother's band room, which is basically Mark's drum set, wall hooks for all his guitars, three old leather couches, a lot of nineties band posters, a big window overlooking the preserve, and what is now probably an antique stack of unopened soda cans.

"Do you hang out up here with your friends?" Shawn asks.

"Not really. It's usually only me and Lucy, and we're always outside or at Lucy's house."

"It's making me want to start a band."

"Mark would love to jam with you. He's probably jamming right now in Brooklyn. I think 'jamming' is his favorite word." I take a bite of chili. "This is delicious. I'm bringing a thermos of this to school every day this week. Mr. Beam is going to be jealous."

Shawn takes out his composting notes. "You know, you could sit with me and my friends. You don't have to eat with Mr. Beam."

"Thanks, but I like the library. It's relaxing."

AT LUNCH

Mr. Beam warms up the chili Shawn and I made in his microwave and then eats most of it himself.

"Hungry, Mr. Beam?" I say.

"Do you want me to waste food, Murphy?"

He has a point.

"Hey, by the way, I found the perfect book for you," he says, grabbing a book from behind his desk. "It's all about climate activism and environmental justice. I loved it. Learned a lot."

"Thanks, Mr. Beam," I say, reading the back cover. "It looks great."

I stick the book in my backpack, leave the delicious-smelling library, and rush down to meet Shawn in the not-delicious-smelling cafeteria to get more pictures of wasted food.

People are talking and shoving and dumping trays of rubbery hamburgers and crinkle-cut fries and fruit cups, only eating ice cream and chips . . . again. We take pictures of the full trash cans and email them to Mr. Lu.

I get a text from Lucy on the way to my locker: **My mom doesn't want to see that doctor. I'm so tired.**

"We have already seen twelve doctors."

"This guy is two hours away, and he doesn't take insurance."

"Let's wait and see if the new meds kick in."

"Let's stick with our plan for now."

"Be patient."

"Be patient."

"Be patient."

OUT OF POCKET

I go straight to Lucy's after school. When I get there, her mom is watering the garden. I don't want to talk to her, because if I do, I might scream, "Why won't you try one more doctor to possibly save your kid, lady?"

I know how parents are. I know how easy it would be for her to say, "You know what, Mary Kate? I'm going to hold off on having visitors for a while so Lucy can rest."

I find Lucy sitting on her floor in her underwear, balancing a history book on her knees and writing in a notebook.

"Hi, Mare." Her voice sounds weak.

"You okay?"

She shakes her head. "I'm giving up. I just keep feeling worse and worse."

"What do you mean?" I sit on the floor across from her.

She tears out a piece of paper, folds it, and hands it to me. "This is my last will and testament. I want you to hold on to it and make sure my parents don't give away all my stuff to my annoying cousin Mikayla."

She crawls into bed and covers herself with the sheet.

I rip the sheet off her. "I'll hold on to it if you go out to the hammock with me. It's cooler out there."

She closes her eyes.

"Come on, Luce. Hammock with me."

She wraps herself in the sheet and shuffles out to the hammock. Her mom's bent over the garden on the other side of the yard.

"I'm not going to let you die, Luce," I say, carefully climbing into the hammock. A few of the leaves on the tree are starting to turn red, and even though things are so bad, for a second I get the warm feeling I always get when fall is coming. "I'll take you to that doctor myself if I have to."

"My parents are constantly complaining about out of pocket."

"What's 'out of pocket'?"

"It's the money they have to pay for my medical bills that insurance doesn't pay. I'd get a job if I could. I don't want to be wasting their money. They already lost the deposits for the bat mitzvah party."

"Aren't you glad you don't have to do that party, though?"

"I'd rather dance in front of the entire school than feel like this."

"Give me a little time to figure this out. There has to be a way to get you to the doctor and pay the out of pocket. You can't die. We have to do our life goals."

"Yeah," she says, from some faraway place.

"Hold on a little longer, Luce. I'm going to help you. I promise."

"Okay, Mare," she says. "I'll try."

It's hard to know what to say to someone who just wrote their last will and testament. I leave her in the hammock, with her head sticking out of the sheet like a mummy, and walk through the preserve.

My best ideas come on walks, but I've got nothing. Maybe that's because *What if she really does die?* keeps popping into my head. I kick the thought into the pond before it has time to take root.

MARY KATE AND LUCY'S LIFE GOALS

- Go to college together.
- Work at the college bookstore, because we know about bookstores.
- Travel to different eco-lodges using our bookstore money.
- Learn the eco-lodge business.
- Get jobs at our favorite eco-lodge after college and make a podcast about it.
- Save money and start an eco-lodge travel agency.
- Own an eco-lodge and live there forever with our families.

HOW OUR ECO-LODGE OBSESSION STARTED

A couple summers ago, Lucy and I were up in Molly's tree house with her dog, Tibby, who we always dog-sit when Molly's at her grandma's. We found a video about an eco-lodge in the Costa Rican jungle, where people could stay without doing damage to the environment. There was a kids' camp where you could learn about plants and animals, and a fruit-bat rehabilitation center, and a forest and farm harvest hike where families could pick their own dinners, and a day trip where you could plant trees.

They had us at *fruit-bat rehabilitation center.*

After we watched the video many times, we looked up eco-lodges all over the world, and our dream was born.

"You don't simply buy an eco-lodge, girls," Dad said when we announced our plan. "You need to study, plan, work, and save, like we did when we dreamed of owning a bookstore."

"We can do that," Lucy said.

Lucy is always optimistic. That's why it's even harder knowing her last will and testament is folded up in my backpack.

LUCY'S LAST WILL AND TESTAMENT

1. *I leave my brother, Blake, my bike, my tradition of making apple crumble pie with Nana at Thanksgiving, my piggy pillow, and all the money in my savings account. (It's up to $1,372 after Nana's check. Please don't waste it on stupid video games. You know I love you, bud.)*
2. *I leave my nana the silver moon necklace she bought me when I was born. It's my favorite piece of jewelry.*
3. *I leave Mom all the books we used to read together and my photo albums.*
4. *I leave Dad my baby bat mug because he always steals it anyway, and my photo of us at the redwood forest.*
5. *I leave all my other stuff to my best friend, Mary Kate Murphy, including our life goals, my bat research binders, and anything I might have forgotten because I don't feel good ATM.*

THE THING ABOUT LUCY'S LAST
WILL AND TESTAMENT

I don't want any of Lucy's stuff unless I can share it with Lucy.

AND NOW IT'S A CLUB

Shawn thought it was a genius idea to invite the whole climate class over to Mark's band room to plan the Applefest booth. The last thing I want to do is have people at my house when I'm so stressed-out about Lucy. But it's too late to cancel now.

I text my brother to ask if I can throw out the band posters. He texts back: **Those are probably worth something. Don't touch them.**

I don't bother arguing. I lug the vacuum and the mop and pail up the back steps of the barn and open all the windows to get rid of the old-shoe smell. I throw tapestries from Sarah's closet over the furniture and hang LED twinkle lights from the Christmas bins. I put apples in a big bowl and pop some popcorn, and the room is as ready as it will ever be.

Shawn shows up first and asks me, "What's wrong?" the second he gets to the top of the stairs.

"Lucy's parents aren't going to take her to Dr. Houlish. They think it costs too much, and they don't want to drive that far."

His face looks as disappointed as I feel.

"I'm so sorry. But I don't think you should give up. Maybe you can get Lucy's mom to talk to my mom. She's really good at convincing people without annoying them. It's definitely her superpower."

"Thanks, Shawn. You've been such a good friend to Lucy and you barely know her."

"I know how hard it is to see someone sick and want to help them get better."

From the window, I see a car pulling up. Ben jumps out and sprints toward the house. I run downstairs and tell him to come to the barn.

Hannah and Rebecca arrive, then Jay, then Elijah, then Rabia. We sit in a circle on the floor and all talk at the same time until Rabia suggests we pass around an apple.

"Whoever holds the apple gets to talk," she says.

This actually works.

"How are we going to make composting less boring?" Rebecca says. "People will pass by our booth yawning. It's not like murals, which are very cool."

"We should dress up in food costumes," Elijah says. "That would be hilarious."

"That would get people's attention," Shawn says.

"Seriously? I don't want to look ridiculous, dressed up like food," Ben says. "Our whole school is going to be there."

"You don't have to do it. It's optional. I'm calling banana, though," Elijah says.

"How are we going to get food costumes?" Rabia asks. "We have less than two weeks to do this."

Hannah raises her hand. "I'll make them. I can sew."

The next half hour is wasted arguing over what foods we should be. Then Mom brings up cider and doughnuts, and we call snack break. Then we argue over who gets to hold the apple next. Hannah gives it to Rabia.

"We should get one of those room dividers with the panels, for all the food-waste information, and we can decorate it with fall colors. We can enlarge the photos of the Fisher trash cans, and on the other side, we can write the vision for what we're hoping to accomplish."

She passes the apple to Jay, who says, "And we can have compost bins with real compost, to show how good it is for people's gardens."

We're all happy with our plan.

Then Hannah holds up her phone. "The mural group is all over Instagram and TikTok," she says. "They're sharing pieces of their project every day until Applefest and asking people to vote for them."

"We need to think of something," Rabia says. "They have the whole high school."

"Posters?" Elijah says. "No, forget it. That's not good enough."

"How about going door-to-door," I say, "like Ms. Lane is doing to get votes?"

"We have thousands of doors in this town," Ben says. "We don't have time for that."

"Whatever, it was just an idea." Then I get one of those light bulbs going off in my head. "We could do a podcast. I did a few this summer, and I know how to do it. We could share it and see what happens."

"Yeah. *Bearsville*. It was good," Jay says. "I really liked the frogs one."

Jay Mendes listened to Bearsville?

"We don't want to bore people," Hannah says. "No offense, but *Bearsville* was kind of boring when the scientist guy was talking for, like, five minutes straight."

Hannah listened to Bearsville *too?*

"I like the idea," Elijah says.

We agree to meet back at the band room on Thursday.

"This can be our climate-club headquarters," Jay says.

"Why does everything need to turn into a club?" I say.

"Because clubs are more fun than classes," Hannah says.

So now, apparently, we're a club.

THE MYSTERIOUS INSTAGRAM POST

Jay takes a picture of us looking like shadowy figures under the twinkle lights and posts it with the caption **Bearsville Climate Club meets at an undisclosed location. Stay tuned for . . . reasons.**

We all share the picture with different captions. Eight people who don't hang out together sharing the same picture at the same time is enough to get a lot of attention at Fisher Middle School. Hopefully, all the curiosity in the comments will get people to listen to the podcast.

Bearsville might not be dead after all.

TEXTS FROM SHAWN

I can't sleep. I'm worried about Lucy. She should have been in Mark's band room with us. She would have had much better ideas than dressing like fruits and vegetables and putting facts on a board. But instead she's lying in her bed all itchy and in pain, with her brain screaming at her like it's on fire.

My phone buzzes from the dresser. I jump up to see if Lucy needs me. But it's a photo from Shawn of a watch.

ME: What's this?

SHAWN: My great-grandfather's pocket watch. His dad was one of the first Black conductors on the train between New York and Boston.

ME: That's so cool.

SHAWN: I want to sell it for Lucy's appointment.

An aching feeling swells up in my chest.

> **ME:** That's very thoughtful of you.
> But let's try some other ideas first.

SHAWN: Okay. But I think it's
worth a lot, and I really want to
do this.

> **ME:** Thank you, Shawn.
> Just thank you.

LETTER TO MY BABY NIECE ON FRIENDSHIP AND OTHER IMPORTANT THINGS

Dear Sweet Pea,

It's two in the morning on a school night, and I can't sleep for many reasons, so I figured I'd write to my favorite baby.

You and your mom are coming this weekend to help with Charlotte's campaign. She's trying to get votes for mayor, and my climate class is trying to get votes for money to do a climate-change project in our town.

I really hope by the time you read this, people have stopped ripping apart the earth for fossil fuels. We can live so much better if we do what we need to do to protect the planet. I don't need to tell you this stuff. Your parents are very smart and have probably already explained it better than I can.

One thing they might not teach you is how to deal with a sick friend. I hope you never have to, but if you do, don't run away or stop seeing your friend, even if they are constantly irritated with you or sleeping most of the time. That's when they need you most. My best advice for being a good friend is to keep showing up, no matter what, and keep believing everything will be okay, even if your friend doesn't.

There's so much more I have to tell you about friendship, but I wanted to get the most important advice down first.

Well, I better try to go to sleep. If you ever can't sleep, find a baby to write a letter to. I'm suddenly extremely tired.

More soon!

Love,
Auntie

ON THE BUS

Molly's sophomore hung out at her house last night.

"What did you do?" I ask, wondering what I would do with someone I like at my house, where he would have to deal with my parents eating pickles and talking about clipped newspaper articles.

She laughs. "We planted mums with my dad."

"No. Seriously."

"Yes. I have proof." She shows me a picture of the sophomore and her dad squatting next to a pile of plants and dirt.

"Did you kiss him?"

"Yeah, Mare. Right in front of my dad and his shovel."

"You'll tell me if you do, right?"

"Of course I'll tell you. I haven't waited this long to kiss someone to keep it to myself. Hey, can I join Bearsville Climate Club?" she says, scrolling through Instagram.

"It's not a real club. We're just trying to get votes."

"I think it should be a real club." She leans over the aisle and tells Will and Talia to like the mysterious Bearsville post. "Maybe our clubs should join together. We're coming up with some good environmental-justice murals."

"If one of us wins the grant, we can talk," I say.

"I bet one of us will win," Molly says. "The mayor was probably hoping nobody would apply so he wouldn't have to deal with it."

"I bet you're right."

THIRD PERIOD

Ms. Lane asks us to describe our happy place, using only nouns and adjectives.

Elijah's is Jamaica, where most of his family still lives.

Rebecca's is Cape Cod.

Hannah's is the horse farm on the other side of Honey Hill.

Jay's is a little island near Puerto Rico.

Rabia's is the mountains of Kashmir, where her grandparents live.

Shawn's is the greenhouse.

Ben's is Lake Placid, in the Adirondack Mountains.

I could say mine is from some family trip we took, or on a beach near my grandma's nursing home, or near Sarah's in Boston. But none of those would be true.

MY HAPPY PLACE

Bear mom. Cubs. Robins. Finches. Cardinals. Catbirds. Fresh nests. Blue eggs. Old nests. Broken nests. Foxes. Coyotes. Jagged rocks. Dragonflies. Pond ripples. Cattails. Tadpoles. Baby turtles. Changing skies. Wildflowers. Sunflowers. Kettle hole. Birch grove. Maple trees. Red leaves. Bats. Dusk. Weeping willow. Me. Lucy. Fairies.

CLIMATE CLASS APPLICATION ESSAY

RABIA MOHAMMED

I think I first understood that climate change is already happening when I went to visit my grandparents in Kashmir two summers ago. The view of the mountains from their little town is so beautiful, and I always remember the tops of the mountains being snowy. When I went two years ago, and also last year, there was so much less snow on the mountains.

My grandmother said she has lived in the town her whole life and has never seen anything like the floods that happened when the glacier melted and caused terrible landslides in a village not that far from her.

I am very worried about climate change. I know people think it's not their concern because it seems like all the worst things will happen a long time from now. But I've seen mountaintops melting with my own eyes, and I know every tiny change has a bigger effect on the whole world.

If you accept me into the climate class, I hope to find ways to worry less about my family and to try to protect their town, and ours as well.

AT LUNCH

"Mr. Beam?"

He looks up from Twitter with a piece of black licorice hanging out of his mouth.

"Yes, Murphy?"

"Do you know any ways to make money quickly?"

"Nothing legal. Why?"

"I need money."

"Have you tried putting up a babysitting flyer?"

Not helpful.

"Good idea. I'll try that."

I wonder what the illegal ways to make money are.

EIGHTH PERIOD

It's like a craft store threw up in Mr. Lu's classroom. It's quiet except for the sound of scissors, and Hannah's sewing machine, and marker squeaking, and Elijah's aggravating humming.

I'm going to be an avocado. My face will be the pit. Hannah says her mom taught her how to sew when she was three. She shows me her Etsy page, where she sells pillows made out of old jeans, with embroidered slogans. Then she measures me for my costume.

Elijah is already wearing the banana costume.

Some kid is staring through the window of the classroom door, so Ben covers it with newspaper.

Mr. Lu, Shawn, and Rabia are working on a budget spreadsheet so we can explain exactly how we would spend the grant money, and everyone else is arguing over how to make the display panels realistic, hopeful, interesting, and informational all at the same time.

Hannah tells me not to move or I'll get stuck with a pin. When she's finally finished, I text Lucy and ask her if I can check on her after school.

She doesn't reply.

WHEN LIFE GIVES YOU LEFTOVER MUFFINS

When Lucy doesn't respond to any of my messages by eight at night, I panic.

I ask Mom to take me over to Lucy's for a minute and say that it's a matter of life and death. She doesn't believe it's a matter of life and death, but she takes me anyway because she wants to drop off leftover zucchini muffins.

When adults don't know how to help a friend, they drop off food.

"Can you explain to Lucy's mom that it makes sense to see Shawn Hill's dad's doctor?" I ask on the way.

"Oh, Mary Kate. It's late. I'm not going to barge in on her right now."

"Whatever," I say, frustrated.

Mom waits in the car while I run up to the front porch. Lucy's mom answers the door and thanks me for the muffins.

"Can I talk to Lucy for a minute?"

"She's asleep, hon."

I almost leave, but then I don't. I need to do whatever it takes.

"Do you think you could talk to my friend Shawn's mom about seeing that immunologist? Dr. Houlish? Shawn says he saved his dad's life."

Lucy's mom looks tired. She has gray hairs sprouting up all over the top of her head and dark puffiness under her eyes.

"Oh, hon. I know you mean well. I really do. But we have this under control. We have to wait and see if the higher dose of anxiety meds works."

My heart speeds up. "How are more anxiety meds going to stop her body from hurting and her skin from itching and all the other symptoms? None of this makes sense."

"Mary Kate, we have been to over a dozen doctors. At some point, we have to stop and trust somebody."

Blake comes down the stairs, grabs the container of muffins, and walks away. Lucy's mom closes the screen door.

I turn away, then turn back. "Is it because the doctor is out of pocket? Because I know Lucy has one thousand three hundred and seventy-two dollars in the bank, and she'll want to spend it if it means she'll feel better."

Lucy's mom opens the screen door and walks out onto the porch. "How did you know Lucy has that much money in the bank?" she whispers.

I freeze.

"I— She probably told me a while ago."

"She couldn't have mentioned it a while ago. Her grandmother gave her an early bat mitzvah gift just last week."

"She . . . I just . . ."

I start crying again, and I turn into a sobbing, shaking pile of kid on the porch floor. Lucy's mom hovers over me, and my mom comes running from the car. My hot tears are dripping on Lucy's mom's bare feet. I crawl on my hands and knees, with my hair stuck to my face, and sit on the porch swing, trying to catch my breath.

Lucy's mom is pacing back and forth.

"She's so sick she thinks she's going to die," I say. I suck in my breath, then breathe out more words I shouldn't be saying. "She wrote her last will and testament. That's how I know what she has in her bank account. It's in her last will and testament."

"Oh no," Lucy's mom says.

She and my mom stare at me like I'm a dog that is about to be put to sleep.

"I don't know how to process this," Lucy's mom says. "It's too hard." She looks at my mom. We all sit on the porch steps. "I keep waking up every day, praying she's better. And sometimes it seems like she's starting to improve. Then she takes a huge tumble. I'm tired of doctors without answers."

My head hurts and I want to go home, but I have to keep trying.

"Please go to one more doctor. He's an immunologist. You haven't tried that kind of 'ologist yet."

She laughs a little. "That's true."

"Shawn's mom said you can call her anytime."

Lucy's mom stands up and wobbles a little as she catches her balance. "You know what, Mary Kate. I'm going to call Shawn's mom right now, okay? I'm heartbroken my baby felt like she needed to write a will."

"Please don't tell her I told you. She'll be mad."

"I won't say anything. Can you text me Shawn's mom's number?"

I do.

She calls.

They talk for two hours.

WHEN NOTHING MATTERS MORE THAN LUCY

By the morning, Lucy has an appointment for Friday at 9:00 a.m. because, according to the receptionist, "We never get cancellations, but we just got one a few minutes ago."

How did this happen? Lucy texts during lunch, while Mr. Beam is reading tarot cards for the new principal in the back office and pretending to have a meeting.

Fairies, I text back.

That's what I thought. Will you come with me? To the doctor?

It's a school day. I have a math test. We have to get ready for Applefest. None of this matters more than Lucy.

Yes.

LETTER TO MY BABY NIECE
ON THE IMPORTANT ROLE OF FAIRIES

Dear Sweet Pea,

Confession. I still believe in fairies. Sometimes I feel them sprinkling magic on me. It gives me courage and wisdom and other things I don't normally have. There are forest fairies. And water fairies. And flower fairies. And there are front porch fairies.

Love,
Auntie

THE BEARSVILLE CLIMATE CLUB PODCAST

ME: I'm Mary Kate Murphy, and welcome to *The Bearsville Climate Club Podcast*. Shawn Hill and I are here to talk about our exciting Applefest grant competition project.

SHAWN: Our Fisher Middle School climate class is excited to teach people in our community about how much food is wasted in America and how food waste is contributing to climate change.

ME: So how much food *is* wasted in America?

SHAWN: From our research, we found out that Americans waste forty percent of the food we buy. More than sixty-six million tons of food are thrown away each year, and most of it ends up in landfills.

ME: Wow. That's hard to even imagine. How does the food in landfills contribute to climate change?

SHAWN: The food decomposes in the landfill, and the decomposition process releases methane into the atmosphere. And methane is an even worse greenhouse gas, in some ways, than carbon dioxide.

ME: So what can we do to reduce food waste?

SHAWN: We can start by not buying so much food in the first place. Only buy what you need. And we can write letters—to restaurants, schools, supermarkets, food courts, and hotels—and ask them to look at how much food they are wasting, and tell them how to use extra food for programs that feed families dealing with food insecurity instead of sending it to the landfill.

ME: That's common sense.

SHAWN: Yes.

ME: Do you have any other suggestions for dealing with food waste?

SHAWN: Yes, I do. We have a very exciting solution, and it has to do with dirt, worms, and other good stuff. If you want to find out what it is, come see the Bearsville Climate Club at the Applefest grant competition in Honey Hill on Saturday, September twenty-fifth, from ten to five. Please stop by our booth. And if you like our project, vote for us!

ME: Thank you, Shawn, and thank you to our listeners.

Jay plays upbeat music.

Rabia raises her hand and says, "And that's a wrap."

"Wow, you were really good," I say to Shawn.

"Thanks," he says.

We share the podcast all over social media.

We tell our parents to share it on Facebook.

And Mr. Lu shares it with everyone in his PhD program, his bicycling club, and his karaoke potluck bird-watching collective, whatever that is.

PIZZA NIGHT

After everyone from climate class leaves Mark's band room, I ride with Mom to pick up Dad from the bookstore, and pizza from the pizza place. When we get to the bookstore, we see somebody waving on the corner near the Congregational church.

"What's that?" I ask Dad as he's locking up.

"Oh, that's Mayor Stuffed Shirt. Standing on the corner with a 'Vote for Me' sign is the closest he'll come to campaigning. And yet people will vote for him."

"Why?"

"Because he promises not to raise taxes, even though he does every year. People don't bother to check."

"Wow."

"He does look sharp in that three-piece suit. That'll pick up a few votes."

"Seriously?"

"Yep. Not a joke, Mary Kate."

THE APPOINTMENT

The car ride on Friday morning almost feels like normal times. Lucy's mom listens to an audiobook, and Lucy and I sit in the way back of the minivan talking about Molly's sophomore planting mums with her dad. Lucy's still skinny and itchy and blinky, and she's dizzy and nauseated from riding in the car, but she's talking and laughing a little.

Does your mom need to use your savings money? I text her.

She looks down at her phone and shakes her head. **No. Aunt Michelle is paying for this. She says she'll do anything to get me better.**

It's always good to have Aunt Michelle on your side.

We watch bat videos the rest of the trip. Bats always seem to calm Lucy down.

When we pull into the parking lot, Lucy's mom lets out a big sigh. "Let's do this," she says.

We wait a long time in the waiting room. Lucy's mom is getting irritated. The receptionist heats something up in the microwave, and the whole office smells like feta cheese, which makes Lucy gag.

"Oh, come on," Lucy's mom says way too loudly.

"Mom, stop." Lucy takes her hands off her face and glares at her mom.

I'm getting more stressed by the minute. There are only so many times I can read the same pamphlet about peanut allergies.

The nurse finally calls Lucy's name.

Lucy pulls me by the arm. "Come on," she says.

The doctor is kind of tall, halfway between my dad and Lucy's dad in age, and he sounds very smart. He asks maybe a hundred questions, and every time Lucy or her mom answers, he says, "Right, right, right"—exactly three times. He examines Lucy, stares at her rashes a while, asks about the blinking and the arm jerking and calls them "tics," and takes a photo of the finger-shaped purple marks on her back and legs. He spends a long time asking about the bottom of her feet.

When her mom brings up her mental health issues and says the word *outbursts* a few too many times, Lucy tells her to never say that word again or she's running away from home.

Dr. H doesn't seem fazed. He reminds me of Father Milt when Pea was screaming during her christening.

"Back to the feet," he says. "Do they burn?"

"Yes. All the time, but really bad in the morning," Lucy says, resting her head on the wall next to the examining table. "Can we take a break?"

Dr. H tells Lucy to get dressed and meet him in his office.

Lucy kicks her mom out and puts on her shorts and her T-shirt. "He asked more questions than all of the other 'ologists combined. And nobody has ever taken pictures of my gross purple marks before."

We meet Lucy's mom and Dr. H in his office and sit in fancy leather chairs.

"Okay, let's see," he says. "I strongly suspect you've got some tick-borne or vector-borne diseases brewing, probably more than one. Infections can cause the immune system to go into overdrive, which may be causing inflammation of the brain, something we call PANS."

"Lucy was tested for Lyme disease early on," her mom says. "And she's never had the bull's-eye rash."

"Many of my patients never had a bull's-eye rash. And most labs don't have the sensitive equipment necessary to diagnose these diseases, so we're going to send your blood to a couple of labs I really trust. Anyway, it'll take a few weeks to get results, but your symptoms are so textbook. The pain, the tics, the brain fog and sudden onset of mood changes, the foot discomfort, the headaches, the striae— those purple marks. Did they crop up with the other symptoms?"

"I think so," Lucy says.

Her mom nods.

"And have you noticed any improvement with the anti-anxiety medication?" Dr. H asks. "I know you recently increased the dose."

"No. None," Lucy says.

"Right, right, right. And considering you spend a good deal of time outside and you have pets, it all adds up."

"So why haven't any of the other doctors suggested this?" Lucy's mom asks.

"That's the million-dollar question," he says. "All I can tell you is I see this all day, every day. I treat with antibiotics and strong herbal antimicrobials, and my patients get better."

"Like, all better?" Lucy says.

"When it's caught early? Absolutely," he says. "Sometimes we need to do some additional therapies, but right now let's see where your blood work leads us." He takes out a lab sheet. "In the meantime, you have the option of starting treatment right away, which I would be okay with, considering your symptoms are so severe and you're missing school. Or you can wait until the blood work comes back."

"I'm not sure I'm comfortable giving Lucy strong antibiotics until the blood work comes back," Lucy's mom says.

Lucy stands up and faces her mom. "It's my body, Mom. I'm not waiting weeks. No way. I'm starting the medicine today."

Lucy gets thirteen vials of blood taken from her arm and then eats a whole sleeve of shortbread cookies with orange juice. While we wait for the antibiotics to be ready, we drive to the beach to lie down flat in the sand and stare up at the cloudless sky.

"You're going to be okay," I tell Lucy. "You know that, right?"

"Yeah. I'm going to be okay."

HONEY

When Lucy's mom drops me off, Sarah and Pea are at our house to help Charlotte knock on doors this weekend. They're going to be coming as much as they can before the election. Sarah wants me to go with her, but knocking on strangers' doors is the last thing I feel like doing.

"It's a beautiful day," Sarah says, snapping Pea into the baby carrier. "Come with me. You can help me if Penelope gets fussy."

"I don't know what to say to people."

"You don't have to say anything. You can stand there and look friendly."

I put on a yellow "Charlotte Lane for Mayor" T-shirt and hold Sarah's clipboard.

We have a local "turf." That means we can walk to the houses where we're door knocking. I'm responsible for handing people the "Come Watch Charlotte Lane Debate Mayor Grimley at Honey Hill High School" flyers.

When we get to the first house, I ring the doorbell. A lady answers, and before we can say anything, she says, "You already have my vote. Have a great day," and shuts the door. Sarah marks her in the yes column, and we go to the next house, where a messy-haired dad carrying a baby about the same age as Pea answers the door, and says, "Oh yeah.

We're all in for Charlotte." They have a boring conversation about baby sleep schedules; then we mark him and his wife as yeses and keep going.

"This is easy," I say.

"I told you," Sarah says.

We get some "Nobody's homes" and hang information on their doors. We get a couple "Not interesteds," and a few more "You have my votes," and one "Didn't we go to high school together?"—which ends up being a twenty-minute trip down memory lane.

The next guy answers the door in shorts. He's not wearing a shirt, and his hairy stomach is sticking out. He takes one look at us and says, "You need to stay in your own lane, honey."

"Excuse me? What is that supposed to mean?" Sarah asks.

"It means you think you can run for mayor when our mayor has been doing this since you were in diapers."

"I'm not running for mayor," Sarah says. "Charlotte Lane is."

"Why don't you go home and take care of your kids, honey. You've got no business being in politics."

He slams the door.

"Aren't you going to say something?" I say, knowing my sister.

"I'm saying a lot of things in my head right now," Sarah says, "but the best way to deal with people like that guy is to get votes for Charlotte."

We keep going.

The very last house is a lady who isn't sure who to vote

for. Sarah tells her about Charlotte and her ability to solve problems and build community. She's so convincing, the lady says, "She sounds terrific. And all these years living here, I've never once had someone for Mayor Grimley at my door. It would be my pleasure to vote for Charlotte Lane."

Pea is fast asleep in her carrier. I wish she knew what was going on so she could see her mom in action.

On the way home, we walk past the shirtless guy's house.

"We're going to win, *honey*," Sarah says.

ON THE BUS

It's Monday morning, and Molly isn't at the bus stop.

Talia helps me with my math homework because she explains things much better than Mr. Parker. The bus comes, and still no Molly.

"She must be sick," I tell the driver.

We turn the corner, and there's Molly, with Bea and Pearl and Navya, and a kid who looks very much like he could be the sophomore, and a crowd of other people. They're holding one big, long sign that says VOTE FOR MURALS AT APPLEFEST. COLOR THE TOWN BEAUTIFUL.

"That's smart," Will says. "Literally every adult drives past this spot on the way to work."

"Yeah, I know," I say.

I take a picture and send it to the climate-class group chat.

Game on, Mr. Lu texts.

I don't know if a podcast is going to get us enough votes, Rebecca says.

People are going to vote for the project they like best, Mr. Lu replies. Just keep doing what you're doing.

AT LUNCH

I'm eating hummus and pita chips, and Mr. Beam is drinking Diet Pepsi and checking Facebook.

"Are you going to show up at Applefest and vote for us?" I ask him.

"I might if I get out of my haircut in time."

"How long is a haircut?"

Lucy's text comes in right before the bell rings. It's a picture of one of those plastic pill cases with morning and night compartments, filled with blue and red pills.

LUCY: Day four.

ME: Pretty pills.

LUCY: Aunt Michelle said to
picture them dissolving in my
body and healing me. It's weird,
but I'm trying it.

I close my eyes and imagine the medicine sliding down Lucy's esophagus, breaking into a million tiny compounds, or molecules, or whatever medicine is made of, and attacking whatever microscopic creatures are living inside my best friend. I picture her filling up with healing energy and growing stronger every day.

"You sleeping, Murphy?" Mr. Beam says.

"No. I'm resting my eyes."

Rebecca texts me: **Are you coming?**

I completely forgot I was supposed to meet her at the end of lunch to take more food-waste pictures.

When I get to the empty cafeteria, Rebecca is sitting on the floor in front of the trash cans, crying, and Sue, our cafeteria lady friend, is standing in front of her looking very confused.

"What happened?" I ask.

"She's upset so many chickens passed away to make the chicken tenders, and now they're in the trash," Sue says. "She's having a tough time, poor thing."

"It's okay. I'll talk to her."

Sue leaves, and I sit on the cold, grubby floor next to Rebecca.

"I'm sorry," I say. "I know how upsetting this is."

Her face is all heartbreak and smeared mascara. "I know people think I'm annoying, but it's so hard. Can I tell you something without you judging me? Because I'm sick and tired of everyone judging me."

"Yeah. I'm not going to judge you, Rebecca."

"I can honestly feel them, the animals. It's like I can feel what they go through. Why can't other people get it? I mean, I completely understand that people are omnivores, and sometimes it's necessary to kill and eat animals. But this?" She points at the trash can. "To kill millions and millions of animals and then care so little you dump them without even eating them?"

"I get it more than you even know. One time, I refused to talk to my dad for a week after he killed a carpenter ant because it was crawling on his newspaper and he thought it was going to nest and eat our house."

She nods. "My mom kills moths for literally no reason. Like, who does that? How do I convince people who don't want to listen?"

"I don't know. I guess that's why we're in climate class. I think you'll figure it out, and it will all make sense."

"I hope so." She looks up at the clock. "I'm sorry I made you late for class. We better go."

"You can go. I'll take the pictures."

"Thanks, Mary Kate."

I take pictures of trash cans full of chicken tenders and green beans and apples.

"Rest in peace, chickens and green beans and apples," I say, and walk as slowly as I can to class.

CLIMATE CLASS APPLICATION ESSAY

REBECCA PHELPS

My name is Rebecca, and I've been a vegetarian since I was six. What does that have to do with climate change? A LOT. I stopped eating meat because I love animals and didn't want to eat them, but then I learned from my neighbor that one of the biggest causes of climate change is all the forests being chopped down to support people's beef obsession. The more trees chopped down for grazing, the fewer trees we have to absorb carbon dioxide. Killing, processing, transporting, and selling animal meat all uses energy. Even cow burps release a lot of methane into the atmosphere. There are many more ways the meat industry contributes to climate change, but these are the big ones. And I personally don't think we should kill innocent animals just for a quick burger.

I would like to learn more about climate change, in general, and how to explain to people that eating as much meat as Americans do is unhealthy—for humans and the planet. My parents didn't want me to stop eating meat, because they eat way too much of it, in my opinion. But they told me I could be vegetarian if I learned to cook my own meals. Now I cook my meals every day, and sometimes when they don't feel like cooking, they eat my meals and admit they're pretty good.

I've been trying to convince everyone I know to stop eating meat, but they mostly ignore me or avoid me. I hope I can attend climate class and learn more about meat and climate change so I can do a better job talking to people about it.

EIGHTH PERIOD

Applefest is three days away, and Mr. Lu is out sick. He promises he'll be back by Friday, but now we're stuck with Mr. Linkler, everyone's least favorite sub.

Jay and Ben go to the art closet to get supplies for the display.

"What are you doing?" Mr. Linkler asks.

"We're doing our project," Jay says.

"No, no, no, no, no. I have the sub lesson plan here. It says you need to take out your textbooks and review chapter eleven."

"We don't have textbooks. That's for a different class," Rabia says.

"This is what I have," Mr. Linkler says.

"What do you have for climate class?" Ben asks.

"I don't have anything for so-called climate class," Mr. Linkler says, "which sounds like a made-up thing."

"We are a special pilot class working on a climate-change curriculum," Rabia tries to explain.

"What are these schools teaching you? Climate change is a figment of some politician's imagination," Mr. Linkler says. "Now take out the book and get to work."

We look at one another, take out random books because we don't have science textbooks, and study our presentation notes for Applefest. We don't know what else to do.

"He's more like the 'missing Link-ler,'" Ben says when Mr. Linkler goes out to the hall to get a drink from the gross water fountain.

He comes rushing back in. "Did you say something?" He points to Elijah.

"No," Elijah says.

"Did you?" He points to Shawn.

"No."

"I heard somebody say something."

"They didn't say anything," I say.

He makes a face and sits in Mr. Lu's chair.

We've wasted an entire period. All we can do is stare at our fake books and hope Mr. Lu gets back here tomorrow.

IN THE HAMMOCK

Lucy's in the hammock when I get to her house after school.

"How are you doing?" I ask, a little afraid to hear the answer. I know Dr. H said it would take a while for the medicine to kick in.

"I'm okay. Last night, I felt really bad, almost like I had the flu. But today my headache is gone, so maybe that's a good sign."

"That's great, Luce."

She pats the hammock, and I slide in next to her. Our tree is getting redder and yellower by the day.

"I can't believe I'm not having my bat mitzvah. My entire family has been planning this thing for months. Years, actually."

"You're just postponing it."

"Not the party. My parents won't book all of that and possibly lose their deposits again."

"We'll do something fun when you're better."

"*If*, Mary Kate. *If* I'm better."

"*When*. And don't fight me."

On my way home, I wander through the preserve, thinking about Lucy and me, and our birthdays being a few weeks apart, and how we always spend them together. I look up at the biggest oak tree, the one with the bright-orange leaves. I decide I'm going to surprise Lucy, not *if* or *when* she gets better, but on her actual birthday. And I have a very good idea.

APPLEFEST CHECKLIST

☑ Make food costumes (Hannah)

☑ Print out photos of food waste (Mary Kate)

☑ Put together food-waste information (Mary Kate)

☑ Put together composting information (Shawn)

☑ Submit application to Town Hall (Mr. Lu)

☑ Decorate panels (Rabia and Jay)

☑ Find tablecloth and make signs (Rebecca)

☑ Post on social media to remind people to stop at our booth (Jay and Elijah)

☑ Get a bucket full of real compost for the table (Ben and Shawn)

☑ Have a meltdown when he gets back from being sick, and stress-eat chocolate (Mr. Lu)

☑ Calm Mr. Lu down, check list one more time, and go home feeling ready—sort of (everyone)

MYSTERIOUS INSTAGRAM POST—PART TWO

Jay posts a picture of a banana, an avocado, a pumpkin, a cucumber, a strawberry, an apple, a piece of celery, and a green bean—us, standing with our backs to the camera, which Ben is holding because he didn't want to wear a costume, so Mr. Lu is now the green bean. Jay tags Applefest and adds the caption: **Who are we? Come find out.**

SWAPPABLE

I wake up at 5:17 a.m. and can't get back to sleep because it's Applefest morning.

I take a shower, try on my avocado costume one more time, and practice my part of the presentation until Dad drives me to the school at eight thirty.

When I get to Fisher, Hannah is waiting in front of the bike rack.

"Hi, Hannah," I say. "Are you excited?" I never know exactly how to start conversations with people I barely know.

"Yeah, but I'm a little nervous. I hope after we get the composting program started, we can do the clothing swap and the other stuff. I feel like that's what I'm supposed to do, like maybe I'll be a sustainable fashion designer someday. I know that sounds stupid."

"It doesn't sound stupid. Can you imagine if you invent a whole brand of clothes made out of hemp or some other perfect plant? Like maybe one we don't even know exists yet?"

"And I could give it a really interesting logo and make it easily coordinated with other pieces so people can swap easily," she says.

"Swappable."

She laughs. "Yeah. Swappable. That could be the name of the brand."

"I love that. But why do you have to wait? Can't you start working on it now? Like those kids who become millionaires before they graduate from high school?"

"Mary Kate, you are so right."

CLIMATE CLASS APPLICATION ESSAY

HANNAH SMALL

I would really appreciate being accepted into the eighth-grade climate class with Mr. Lu because I know Mr. Lu is an excellent teacher, and I am very interested in how fast fashion is damaging our planet and how we can change our fast-fashion habits.

For example, I found a shirt in the back of my closet that I never ended up wearing. That shirt made quite the journey to get to my closet. It started as cotton in a field, which took a lot of water and pesticides to grow. Then it was shipped all the way across the world to get to a factory, where it was turned into fabric, and then it was shipped to another country to be dyed. The people in those factories worked in horrible conditions so my shirt would be cheap. It was so cheap I didn't even bother to wear it. Eventually, that shirt will go to a landfill, where it will decompose and release methane gas into the atmosphere.

There's no way we can continue buying so much cheap clothing without huge problems. I watched a documentary about fast fashion and then looked up a lot of articles for a report I did last year, and I found out that all of the stores I liked the most were fast-fashion clothing stores.

I love shopping and clothes. But I don't want to destroy the planet just so I can have new outfits. So I started a clothing swap with my friends.

I would like to study sustainable fashion someday, and I know learning more about climate change will be so helpful for my future career and my life. Please consider me for the climate class.

ROTTEN APPLES

Everybody starts showing up. Mr. Lu waves us over to his Subaru, and we carefully move the display from our classroom to the car. A few parents drive us all to the fairgrounds, and we put on our fruit and vegetable costumes in the parking lot.

There are five booths in the big blue tent. That means we have four competitors, a few more than we thought, but not that bad. Ben's dad goes around asking the people setting up what their proposals are about. He comes over to us and reports:

There's the artificial-turf-for-the-high-school-field booth.

The new-addition-to-the-food-pantry booth.

The new-signs-at-the-bike-path-trailhead booth.

The social-justice-club-mural booth.

And an empty booth for us.

Molly, Bea, Olivia, and Navya are setting up the mural booth. They have stands with miniature mural mock-ups.

"This looks so good," I say.

"Thanks, Mare," Molly says.

Shawn and I set up our panel display behind the empty table. We cover the table with a rust-colored tablecloth and scatter leaves on top.

A woman in high-heeled boots and a fur-collared jacket comes rushing toward us. "Who's in charge here?" she asks.

"Mayor Grimley, I think?" Rabia says.

"No, I mean who is in charge of your group?"

We look at Mr. Lu. "Can I help you?" he asks.

"This is our booth," she says, holding up a paper.

"I'm sorry," Mr. Lu says, "but I think you're mistaken."

"We're booth three. This is booth three," the woman says. "My colleague is unloading the truck, so we really need to figure this out."

I'm getting a bad vibe from the lady.

"Let me go straighten this out with the mayor," Mr. Lu says.

Molly and Bea come over. "What's wrong?"

"We don't know," I say. We're not sure if we should keep setting up or not, so we stand in a circle, staring at one another.

Mr. Lu is over in the corner of the tent. He's a grown man in a green-bean costume, waving his hands at the mayor and getting more red-faced by the minute. Then the mayor walks away, and Mr. Lu comes back looking completely stunned.

"I—I don't even know what to say. This is unbelievable."

"What's wrong, Mr. Lu?" Elijah asks.

"He . . . They apparently left a message with the secretary at school the day I was out—which I never got—and said that because not all the students in our class live in Honey Hill, we're disqualified from the grant competition."

Shawn is the only kid in the class who doesn't live in Honey Hill.

"But he goes to school here," I say. "Did you explain that to him?"

Mr. Lu shakes his head. "They're saying everyone on the application must be a resident of the town. Otherwise, we can't participate. I—I'm so sorry. I had no idea."

We can't move. We're in shock.

Shawn's face drops. He rips off his costume and walks out of the tent.

I text Sarah: **Please come right now.**

She comes rushing into the tent with Ms. Lane, and we all start talking at once.

"This is utterly unacceptable," Ms. Lane says. "Shawn is a student in this district. He belongs on this team."

The fur-collar lady comes back in with her colleague, who's carrying a SNACK CARTS FOR TWIN HILLS GOLF CLUB sign. He also gives me a bad vibe.

"So we're being pushed out by people who want snack carts at a golf club?" Rebecca says. "I can't believe this is happening."

Jay comes running into the tent, pulling his pumpkin costume over his soccer uniform. Hannah tells him what's happening, and Jay tells his dad, who is a lawyer. His dad huddles outside the tent with Mr. Lu and then comes over to tell us what we don't want to hear.

"They can do pretty much anything they want with this type of thing," he says. "Sorry, guys. This is tough stuff."

"This is racism," Molly says. "I'm telling you right now.

How much more do the students from Hartford need to deal with?"

I hadn't thought of it that way.

Ms. Lane nods. "She's absolutely right. How are we giving students an equal education if they can't even participate in community activities without being punished for their zip code?"

Jay's dad, Mr. Lu, Sarah, and Ms. Lane go outside, to talk to the mayor some more. The superintendent, Dr. Eastman, joins them and hovers about an inch away from the mayor's face. We stand in a circle again, now holding our display, because the fur-collar lady is using the only empty table.

They come back, and Jay's dad says, "He's not budging."

We don't have a choice. We have to go.

We weave through the crowds of sticky caramel-apple kids and their bored parents. Bees are everywhere, drunk on sugar. I'm so mad I feel like stinging someone, hornet-style.

We're embarrassed and furious and heartbroken at the same time. We let our parents load the panels into Mr. Lu's Subaru as, together in our ridiculous costumes, we watch from the edge of the parking lot.

"We need to go find Shawn," Elijah says.

"He left with his mom," Ben says.

I text Mom and Dad not to bother coming, and wait for Sarah, who's getting apple fritters.

Hannah's crying. "I'm just so mad," she says.

"I want everyone to huddle," Mr. Lu says.

We huddle.

"Listen, we are bigger and better than this bogus Applefest grant. We have a vision," he says. "I want you to picture that bulletin board in our classroom. We wouldn't be real climate scientists if we didn't meet resistance, right? It's going to light a fire under us and make us work harder."

"How, Mr. Lu?" Jay asks. "We're not going to have money for composting at the school."

"We are going to figure it out. The first rule of climate club is: 'Expect adversity and work around it.' Now let's go home and regroup. Think about our vision and how we're going to make it happen."

"What about Shawn?" I ask. "He must feel horrible."

"I'll reach out to Shawn," Mr. Lu says, "but it would be great if some of you could as well."

We walk toward our families, who are standing awkwardly between the parking lot and the Applefest entrance. Out of the corner of my eye, I see a group of people moving toward us.

"Hey, climate class," Navya yells. "Wait a second!"

It's the social-justice club. They're carrying their Social Justice Club banner and the miniature murals.

"We quit," Molly says.

"What do you mean?" I ask.

"We left. We're not participating in their racist grant contest," Bea says. "Check your phones. We made a little scene."

THE LITTLE SCENE (AS SEEN ON TIKTOK)

"I'm Molly Frost, and I'm here with the Honey Hill High School Social Justice Club, where Mayor Grimley has just kicked the Fisher Middle School climate class out of the Applefest grant competition because one of the students in the class happens to live in Hartford."

Molly walks over to the mayor.

"Mayor Grimley," she says, "can you explain why you kicked out the Fisher Middle School climate class after they have been working on this for weeks?"

"The rules were clear," the mayor says. "All participants must be Honey Hill residents."

"Are you aware of the fact that students who come here from Hartford are Honey Hill students?"

"Yes. I left a message at the school explaining the situation."

"This is such obvious racism," somebody yells from the other side of the camera.

The mayor whips his head around. "Oh, come on. That's out of hand. Are you taping this?"

"You're the mayor. You could change the rule right now if you wanted," our friend Liza says. "I live in Hartford. If I had written my name on the application, we'd be disqualified too."

"I can't change the rule. It would require a town council

resolution," the mayor says. "I apologize for the mix-up in communication, but can we please move along?"

"We're out of here," Molly says.

"Grimley is wrong," somebody yells.

They all start chanting, "Grimley is wrong!"

The video ends.

There are already seven hundred views.

THE SALAD MAN

Sarah drives me to Hartford. She takes Pea for a walk in the stroller, and I find Shawn in the greenhouse, picking salad greens to deliver to elderly people around his neighborhood.

"I'm fine," he says. "Why is everyone checking on me?"

"Because it was so messed up, and you're as much a part of our community as anyone."

"We probably should have looked at the application more carefully."

He's acting strange.

"Can you stop picking stuff for a second?"

"People are expecting deliveries."

"They can't be expecting them right now, because we were supposed to be at Applefest."

He stops and stares at me. "What's up, Mary Kate?"

"Can we sit?"

We sit at the little white table.

"Fritter?" I say, pulling the greasy paper bag out of my backpack.

"No, thanks. My mom got us some."

Silence.

"It smells like worms in here," I say.

"It's the compost."

"Oh yeah. Right."

Silence.

"Shawn, I want to say I'm sorry all this happened. Mr. Lu says that climate scientists always have to face issues, and we're going to keep going, so—"

"I'm sick of it. I've been going to school in that town since kindergarten, and I'm still just a Hartford kid," he says. "We get ignored so often we're numb to it. I don't want to be numb, but I am. I mean, would it be that hard to get invited to a birthday party? Why is it okay to sit in class with us every day but pretend we don't exist outside of school? I don't get it."

I feel horrible. "I'm sorry."

"Can we forget about this? I've dealt with a lot worse. Like the time I swung at a kid for calling my sister the n-word when she was five years old and *I* got punished. That was fun. Do you think it's easy to go into the bathroom at school and stand there and pee in front of a group of kids calling me the worst words you could imagine?"

"Oh, Shawn."

"And my cousin in college? How many times did people ask if they could touch her hair? Like, who does that? And I still remember all of her white Honey Hill friends asking if she wanted to go with them and their dates to the prom because the kid she liked told everyone he wasn't 'into Black girls.' She never told her parents. She just cried in her room and said she wasn't a prom person."

"I don't know what to say."

"There's not much to say." He puts on his gardening gloves and stands up. "Can you help pick some greens?"

He gets a pair of gardening gloves off the shelf for me and shows me how to do it. We pick greens, and listen to music, and divide the greens into bunches, and then walk from house to house with Sarah and Pea and Shawn's sister, Sydney.

"Hi, Mrs. Vega. Salad time," Shawn says.

"Hey, Mr. R. Salad time," he says at the next house.

"Shawn's the salad man," Sydney says.

"I see that," I say.

WALLS

On the way home, Sarah pulls over in a library parking lot a couple blocks away from Shawn's to feed Pea, whose crying is disturbingly loud. I take a picture of an amazing mural on a building next door and send it to Molly.

"I have to get home," Sarah says. "I'm helping Charlotte start to prepare for the Grimley debate. She's going to take him down with words."

We buckle Pea into her car seat.

"Sar," I say, "I get how Molly's club was saying the Applefest grant rule was racist, but I don't know how to explain why it was racist."

"Systemic racism is when a whole system is set up on a foundation of racism. Stuff like housing laws, town ordinances, and rules like the one for the Applefest grant uphold that system of racism. If people aren't actively thinking about how to *not* be racist when they make laws, the laws often slide right back into that foundation, like cement drying on top of a wall. The town council may not have thought, 'Let's exclude Black students from our grant process,' but they didn't actively think of the mostly Black students with out-of-district addresses when they designed the grant. That's systemic racism. Does that make sense?"

"It makes sense," I say. "But the mayor could have said, 'We didn't think of that, and we're going to change the rule to include students from Hartford.'"

"Yep. But he didn't."

"Charlotte would have."

"That, my dear sister, is why we're trying to get her elected."

LETTER TO MY BABY NIECE ON MY BIGGEST HERO

Dear Sweet Pea,

I would like to tell you about your mom because now that you're twelve, she might be annoying you and embarrassing you by blasting her old music and car dancing when she drops you off at school. (I get it.) But I want you to know that your mom is the strongest and smartest person I know. Uncle Mark is fun, and your dad is super nice and really good at engineering and comic book collecting and other things you'll appreciate, but your mom is wise. It's like she has lived a thousand lives and now she finally understands what most people don't. She's brave too. She's not afraid of anything. Except getting hit by a baseball at a game. But who isn't? She is an amazing role model to me, and I love her so much. You are a very lucky baby (twelve-year-old).

Love,
Auntie

CLUBS

ME: The social justice club TikTok has 12,000 views.

MOLLY: I know, and a lot of evil comments.

ME: Don't read the comments.

MOLLY: The golf club people got the grant.

ME: I think I'm going to throw up.

MOLLY: Join the club.

WHEN LUCY MEETS PEA

Sarah's stressed-out when Mom says she's not missing mass and Dad says he doesn't trust himself with a newborn.

"What? You've had three newborns," Sarah tells Dad.

"Those were my own."

"Okay," she says to both of them, "so I have to cancel helping Charlotte because *you* have church and *you* have incompetence?"

"I'll babysit," I yell from my bed.

Sarah says I can put Pea in the baby carrier and walk her around the preserve as long as I walk slowly and don't get distracted looking at birds.

I strap her in tight and stick the bottle of milk Sarah pumped out this morning in my backpack. I take tiny shuffle steps through the bushes and stop at the end of the path.

"Pea, this is the preserve," I say in a baby voice. "Your mom and Uncle Mark and I grew up here, and you will too."

We walk through the fairy forest, and I show her the remnants of the fairy-house village Lucy and I spent so many hours building over the years.

"There's magic here, Pea," I whisper. I stand still for a minute. "If you're quiet, you can hear the fairies flying through the trees. They're very fast and *very* beautiful. And they will protect you wherever you go."

She stops making her grunting sounds, and I actually think she might understand me. We listen. To the creaking tree limbs. To the forest, rustling like a living being.

Then we shuffle all the way to Lucy's.

Aunt Michelle is visiting again.

"Oh. Give me that baby," Aunt Michelle says, practically yanking Pea out of the carrier.

"I hope you can help me put her back in this carrier thing," I say, running up to Lucy's room.

She's awake and sitting up in bed.

"Luce, I brought a surprise."

"Wait, Mare, tell me what happened yesterday. I was ready to go surprise *you* and vote for climate class, and then I saw Molly's video."

"It was so bad, Luce. The whole Applefest thing was a mess."

"We should do our own festival. Applefest was always boring anyway, except for the fritter truck."

"That's true. The fritters are the only good thing there," I say. "Come see my surprise."

Lucy follows me downstairs. Aunt Michelle holds up Pea, and Lucy smiles bigger than I've seen her smile in a long time.

WHEN I MET LUCY

I met Lucy in a mud puddle.

We were almost seven, and she had just moved to Honey Hill from New York City. It was pouring that day, and the gym teacher opened the gym doors to give us some air because we were sweaty from playing kickball.

I snuck outside for a minute to jump in a puddle, which ended up being deeper than I thought. It soaked my pants up to the shins. But I kept jumping.

After a few minutes, I felt a splash go all the way up my back. I turned, and there she was: a girl about my size with two missing front teeth and soggy brown curls.

I'd finally found someone who loved puddle jumping as much as I did.

Mom makes me my favorite meal in the universe, fettucine Alfredo. We eat out on the porch because it's warm for
the end of September, and fettucine tastes even better, for
some reason, when we eat it outside.

Sarah and Pea went back to Boston a little while ago,
and I never thought I'd miss a screaming baby so much.
Dad brings out the bread, and the three of us twist fettucine
on our forks and dunk the bread in the Alfredo sauce.

"It's such bad luck that the stuffed-shirt mayor threw
a wrench into your climate-class project," Mom tells me.
"You kids worked so hard on that."

"It was more than a wrench, Mom. It was racism."

"That's a little harsh, isn't it?" Dad says. "I mean, it
seems like it was one of those rigid-rules things."

I feel my hornet-attack pheromone firing up.

"Do you think it's a coincidence that the Hartford
kids"—I pause to correct myself—"the students from Hartford, who are almost all Black, are never really included in
this community?"

"I see what you're saying," Mom says. "I simply don't
know if disqualifying your team was purposefully racist.
That's all."

"Does an action have to be on purpose in order for it to be racist?" I say. "Or can it just be racist because it's continuing a racist system?"

"You don't need to yell, Mary Kate," Dad says. "You sound like your sister."

"Good. My sister is usually right." I get up to leave. "Maybe you should actually read some of those books on your Black Lives Matter display at the store."

"Go to your room, Mary Kate," Dad says. "Now."

"I'm going." I grab my fettucine and go inside.

Another thing about having old parents is they love to say, "Go to your room."

I try to call Sarah, but she's probably still driving.

I text Shawn: **Can you call me?** I don't feel like Face-Timing. I want to lie under the covers in the dark.

He texts back: **Yeah.**

We talk for two hours. I don't tell him about my parents, because they're embarrassing, but I tell him about my talk with Sarah.

"I really want to start a climate club in Hartford," he says.

"Why don't you?" I say.

"I don't even know how to begin. Mr. Lu has a fancy grant to pay for our climate-class pilot program. Who's going to pay a teacher in my neighborhood to start a class or run an after-school club?"

I don't have an answer.

"It makes me furious that my little sister wants to go to a boarding school because she thinks maybe she'll finally be accepted there," Shawn says. "She's obsessed with all-white shows about boarding schools. But like, why can't we go to school in our own neighborhood and have all the 'resources'—whatever that means—here?"

"Why is that, actually?"

"I don't know. And most teachers at Fisher don't get it—I mean, other than Mr. Lu and Ms. Lane and a few others. It's so frustrating that most of the staff at our school are white, except one Chinese guy, a Puerto Rican counselor, and a Black custodian."

"Wow. I've never thought about that."

"You haven't had to think about that. You don't have to think about the stuff I have to think about. I'm constantly worrying about how to be seen and heard through all the white noise. I have to think, 'Gee, Shawn, should you walk over to the pizza place after school, or is somebody going to think you're a robber and call the cops? I mean, you're hungry, but maybe it's worth waiting until you can go to a pizza place near home, because one day that person calling the cops could get you murdered,' " he says. "I'm tired, Mary Kate."

I'm angry at my parents, and our school, and our town, and myself, for not considering how the kids like Shawn must feel every single day.

"Can you do me a favor?" he asks.

"Definitely."

"Why are you saying 'definitely' when you don't even know what the favor is? What if I ask you to eat a baby animal or something?"

"I *definitely* trust that you won't ask me to do something so horrifying."

"Can you not act weird? Can you not be extra nice because I told you all that?"

"I won't act any weirder than I usually act."

He laughs. "I'm going to bed."

"Good night, Shawn."

MY LETTER TO MAYOR STUFFED SHIRT

Dear Mayor Grimley,

With all due respect, I'm emailing you to formally complain about the way you handled the entire grant competition at Applefest.

I feel you could have changed the rules or made an exception for a student attending a school in the district. You had a lot of power over the situation, and you decided to kick out a class of eighth graders who worked really hard on their project.

Whether you are aware of this or not, your action was unfair and, to be honest, racist. The rule excluded a Black student from participating in town events because he didn't have a Honey Hill address. If you were interested in NOT being racist, you would have made sure the rules were fair to everyone in our community, including the kids who go to school here.

I know it's too late for this year, but I suggest you consider changing your policies to include students at Honey Hill schools who may not be residents. This will make everyone feel welcome at events like Applefest.

I also think apologizing would go a long way.

> *Sincerely,*
> *Mary Kate Murphy*
> *Grade 8,*
> *Fisher Middle School*

AT THE BUS STOP

I avoid my parents, who are hovering over their oatmeal and their newspapers. Molly and Will are already at the bus stop.

"Gross," Molly says. "Mrs. Caldwell has a 'Reelect Grimley' sign. What is she thinking?"

"And why do his signs have American flags on them?" Will asks. "He's not running for president."

"He thinks he is," Molly says. "He reminds me so much of Couchman."

Dr. Couchman was the principal at Fisher last year, who carried around a laminated copy of our school dress code and harassed people for wearing perfectly normal clothes.

"Except Grimley is fake nice," I say, "which makes it easy to trick people."

"People like Mrs. Caldwell," Will says.

"Pearl says we should say things we want to happen in the present tense and send it into the universe," Molly says. "It's called an intention."

"I'll try anything," I say.

"Charlotte Lane wins in a landslide," Molly says.

Charlotte Lane wins in a landslide.

I say it over and over again in my head until the first bell rings.

EIGHTH PERIOD

We're all tired and frustrated, and nobody has any good ideas for what to do now that we're not sitting here with $10,000 for a school composting program. So Mr. Lu takes us out the window and lets us sit in the Kindness Garden, staring at the changing leaves and letting the sun warm our brains.

Climate club might actually be turning into a real club. I thought it would disappear after Applefest, but people keep coming up to us, asking if they can join. When we asked him, Mr. Lu said, "The first rule of climate club is: 'The more the merrier.'" But I don't know if that's true. Why should we be recruiting new people if we don't know what we're doing?

Shawn and I sit under my favorite birch tree and try to think of a way to get our composting program going without money.

"We could try to compost on our own, like out here near the woods," Shawn says. "I've studied how to do it, and it's not that hard."

"Don't you think it would be hard with so much waste?" I say. "And what if we get bears or a gross rat infestation? Then people might be totally turned off by the whole thing."

"That is very true."

When Mr. Lu leans out the window and rings his wind chimes, Shawn and I climb back into the classroom with nothing to share.

"Okay, what've you got?" Mr. Lu asks the class.

Rabia raises her hand. "We should think of a fundraiser, maybe something that can raise money and educate people in the community at the same time."

People suggest a whole list of ideas, but they're rejected because they're boring or they'll probably somehow contribute to climate change:

Bake sale.

Car wash.

Selling candy bars.

Selling nature photography calendars.

Golf tournament.

"You know," Mr. Lu says, "we could go back to my idea of educational bulletin boards at all the schools."

"No," we all say at the same time.

"I think we should protest what happened at Applefest in front of Town Hall," Jay says. "The mayor shouldn't get away with this."

"He might be gone in a few weeks," Rebecca says.

"And he might not," Jay says.

"I think we should do something bigger," Shawn says. "Something epic."

"Okay," Mr. Lu says. "Your homework is to sleep on this and come back with epic."

THE ANIMAL GRAVEYARD

When my brother, Mark, comes home, he spends most of his time mountain biking down the sledding hill, even though he's thirty-four years old. He's not Sarah, but he gives me good pieces of advice. He likes to call them wisdom nuggets. I'm using one of them today: When Mom and Dad are mad, bring some friends home. They'll be too polite to yell at you in front of them. They'll pretend everything is normal so they can avoid whatever conflict you're having.

Shawn and Sydney come home with me after school. We're waiting for Molly and Navya to show up for a pop-up podcast. Navya is bringing a recording that has something to do with the Applefest incident.

Mom is at the computer doing bookstore inventory when we get to my house, soaked from the rain that came out of nowhere. I give Shawn and Sydney towels to dry off, and Mom offers them soup and warm bread.

Sydney seems very comfortable at the kitchen table doing her homework. The rain is finally slowing down, and sun streams through the big window in the kitchen.

"Do you want to go to the preserve?" I ask.

"No, thank you," Sydney says. "I've got stuff to do."

"You okay if we go?" Shawn says.

"Why wouldn't I be?" Sydney says. "Unless you have ghosts here or something."

"Not that I know of," I say, grabbing my binoculars and sticking them in my backpack.

We leave Sydney slurping soup and asking Mom if she has ever had any ghost encounters in this old house.

We don't say much on the way to the sledding hill. We walk with Claudia and Murphy, and think, and listen to the birds.

"If I show you something," I say, "do you promise not to make fun of me?"

"I can't promise," Shawn says, "but I'll try."

"Seriously, Shawn. Lucy and I are the only ones who know about this."

"Okay, I won't make fun of you. And now I really want to know."

We slide down the wet grass to the bottom of the hill, and I lead him toward the fairy forest between the preserve and Lucy's house. I count eleven trees up and fourteen to the left, and we duck under a mess of brambles.

"Be careful of the pricker monsters," I say.

"Ow."

"I told you to be careful."

The sun is out now, warming the forest in soft end-of-day light.

"We're here," I say.

"What is it?" Shawn asks, looking at the mounds of rocks dotting a clearing.

"It's an animal graveyard. Actually, it's our animal grave-yard. Lucy and I buried all these creatures ourselves."

"Really? What kinds of animals are we talking about?"

"Birds, squirrels, chipmunks, an opossum. The saddest one was a baby deer. Oh, and Lucy's murdered chicken. A fox got her. Her dog chased the fox away, but it was too late for Pretty. That was her name."

"Where did you find them all?" He leans down and touches one of the grave markers.

"Different places. Most of them were sick or injured when we found them. Some we tried to help, but they didn't make it."

We weave through the animal tombstones, stopping at each one.

"It's sad," Shawn says.

"Too sad to describe." I tell him about the mother robin, jumping frantically next to her baby, who had fallen out of the nest. "We gave them nice funerals—with music and poems and stuff."

"That's good."

We stand for a few minutes.

"Thank you for taking me here," Shawn says. "I would never make fun of something like this."

"I know."

On our way home, I see a flash of black. I assume it's Mrs. Caldwell's Lab, who is always escaping her invisible fence. But then Claudia starts barking, and I know it's the bears.

"Shawn, look," I whisper, and I point.

"No way. No way." He freezes.

"It's the mom and her two cubs. They've grown a lot. They're teenagers now."

"This is incredible. But do you think they could come after us? Like charge at us?"

"Nah. They're on their way to bed."

We stand at the base of the sledding hill and watch them lumber across the meadow and into the forest on the other side of the pond. The sun is starting to set, and Sydney is texting us to get back to my house because Dad is asking her boring questions and she needs to get her homework done.

"I think I *am* going to start the climate club in my neighborhood," Shawn says. "I don't really need money to start it. I just need help telling people about it."

"I'm so glad you're doing this. I'll help you any way I can."

"Thanks, Murphy."

We walk a while, and then Shawn says, "Did you ever think it might not be a good idea to handle dying animals?"

"No," I say. "First responders don't think that way."

When we get back, Navya and Molly are in my kitchen with Sydney and Dad. We go out to Mark's band room, and Navya plays the recording she got from a kid whose dad was running the bike-trail-sign booth at Applefest.

We play it again and again.

"Not surprised," Sydney says. "At all."

THE BEARSVILLE CLIMATE CLUB PODCAST

EPISODE TWO

ME: This is Mary Kate Murphy, and welcome to *The Bears-ville Climate Club Podcast*. Today we're hosting a special episode. We're talking to two students from the Honey Hill High Social Justice Club, Molly and Navya. They're here to share some information they've received about the incident at the Applefest grant competition. Molly, would you like to give us some background on what you saw that day?

MOLLY: Yes, we were planning to display our mural project at the grant competition when we witnessed Mayor Grimley reject your climate-class project because one of your classmates is not a resident of Honey Hill, even though he is a student at Fisher Middle School. Our social-justice club decided to walk out. We didn't want to be part of what we believed to be an unfair and racist situation.

ME: I know many listeners have seen the TikTok of you confronting Mayor Grimley that day. But Navya has new information we want to share.

NAVYA: Yes, we received a video from someone who was also in the tent that day but would like to remain anonymous. They were recording when we were doing the

TikTok and continued recording after we left the tent. I'm going to play the recording now.

She presses Play. We hear muffled voices and then:

FIRST MAN'S VOICE: Those kids were out of line. Typical, entitled, coddled.

SECOND MAN'S VOICE (SOUNDS LIKE THE MAYOR): If I make an exception for that kid, we'll have inner-city folks coming out of the woodwork, sniffing around for money.

FIRST MAN'S VOICE: *[Laughter.]* Ain't that the truth?

We hear more muffled voices, and the recording shuts off.

HOW TO MAKE A PODCAST GO VIRAL

Play a never-before-heard really offensive sound bite of your mayor.

SARAH HAS WISDOM NUGGETS TOO

I call Sarah and tell her what happened with the recording, and that Mom and Dad are still giving me the silent treatment after our fettucine-night fight. Sarah tells me I need to speak their language if I want to get through to them.

"What's their language?" I ask.

"Articles," she says. "Print out a pile of articles on implicit bias and systemic racism. Trust me, it'll be worth the wasted printer paper. Put them in a folder and give it to them with a smiley-face note and two cups of chamomile tea."

"You're good," I say.

"I've been around the block."

Before bed, I print out a few articles Sarah texted me, paper-clip them, and slide them into a blue folder, with a sticky note that says *I'm sorry for losing my temper. I hope you'll read these. I love you.*

I put the folder and two cups of tea on Mom's nightstand while they're taking out the garbage and recycling.

In the morning, they still act like nothing happened, but the folder is on top of their pile of newspapers.

I'm going to take that as a good sign.

EIGHTH PERIOD

Mr. Lu collects our "Natural Gas Is a Nice Way of Saying 'Methane'" homework and points to the floor, which means it's sit-in-a-circle time. He turns off the lights, and we sit, listening to the rain pelt the windows.

"Before we begin," Mr. Lu says, "I want to remind you, once again, that we started the school year with a vision, and while it would have been nice to have that grant money, we have work to do and time is ticking. So let's throw some stuff out and see what sticks."

Elijah raises his hand. "I think we should keep doing the podcast. I had a lot of people come up to me and tell me they listened. And I mean people from outside this school. So it's a good way to spread the word about what we're doing."

"Now we're cooking," Mr. Lu says. "I'll even let you do the podcasts in class if you want."

"Speaking of cooking, I was thinking we could do a project about how meat consumption contributes to climate change," Rabia says. "Rebecca could share her recipes."

"What recipes? Rebecca has recipes?" Mr. Lu says.

Rebecca nods. "I've been working on a cookbook. My

parents told me if I go vegetarian, I have to cook for myself, so I have a lot of recipes."

"Now *that* might get people interested in cutting out meat," Mr. Lu says. "You don't have to force it down their throats. You just need to feed them delicious ideas."

"She made me vegan pizza after school the other day," Rabia says. "It was delicious."

"I want vegan pizza," Elijah says.

"I'll make it for you whenever you want," Rebecca says.

"What about our other projects, though?" Hannah says. "I really want to do the clothing swap."

I get a flash of something Lucy said the other day.

"Hey, Lucy had an idea," I say.

"Yeah, and . . . spit it out," Ben says. He can be so annoying.

"What if we have our own festival?" I say. "A not-boring one. I mean, has anyone ever cared about going to Applefest before this grant thing? Other than to get fritters and leave? It's pretty much just businesses in booths giving out free pens, and one dirty inflatable slide. They don't even have normal music."

"That is true," Rabia says.

"We could have our own festival and charge money, and do the clothing swap and other stuff," Rebecca says. "I love that. What if we do it Halloween weekend?"

"And then we could do the electric-vehicle show in the parking lot. And give out information about idling," Elijah says. "I like this plan."

"And we could have the company we want to use for the

composting at school set up a booth to teach everyone how composting works," Shawn says.

"Do you think we could get a band?" Jay asks. "Or a DJ?"

"People are talking about trying to have a Halloween dance," Hannah says. "What if we have a dance the night of the festival and ask everyone to wear handmade or repurposed costumes?"

"Whoa, whoa, whoa. I gotta say, these are pie-in-the-sky ideas," Mr. Lu says. "You realize Halloween is a month away, right? This festival of yours would take a heck of a lot of work. And then to do a dance the same night? I don't know if we could pull it off. I mean, maybe we could . . . if we hired DJ Dizzy Lu."

"Oh boy, here we go," Jay says. "Is this the part where you only agree to help us if we let you DJ?"

"Let me? You'll have to beg me. I'm only the best DJ in the Mr. Beam party circuit."

"Are there zero-waste fritters?" Elijah says. "We have to have fritters."

We get up.

We turn the lights on.

We draft a plan on the smartboard, and DJ Dizzy Lu sends a text to schedule a meeting with the superintendent, who he claims is now his best friend after they hung out at the staff cookout last night.

"We need a name for this festival," I say.

Shawn raises his hand. "How about Funfest? Like the opposite of Applefest. Or maybe the Bearsville Climate Club Fall Funfest."

"I like it," Ben says. "It's like fun, but also fall, and then you also mention climate club."

"Act professional," Mr. Lu says, looking down at his phone. "The superintendent already texted me back. She's in the building right now, and on her way here this very minute."

Mr. Lu opens the door for Dr. Eastman. Her hair is now bright blue, and her heels are candy-apple red.

"I can't tell you how excited I am that Fisher is doing this climate class," she says. "It's going to be so inspiring to see what y'all come up with. I'll do whatever I can to support your work, so tell me what you have in mind."

We all look at Mr. Lu.

"We don't quite have a polished plan, but we'll share our basic vision and let you know what we need—if that works for you."

He seems a little nervous.

"Sure does," she says. "Let's hear it."

Mr. Lu points to Rabia, the calmest presenter in the class.

"We want to have our own festival," she says. "It's kind of soon, but we're hoping to do it Halloween weekend here at Fisher. We're thinking about zero-waste refreshments, a compost demonstration tent, a clothing swap, and Elijah had a great idea." She looks at Elijah.

"We want to have car dealers bring over electric cars and have an electric-car show. We could also have anti-idling information and a booth about how bad leaf blowers are for the environment."

"And then a dance at night for Fisher students," Hannah adds, "with Mr. Lu as the DJ."

When it's presented in one, big chunk, it does sound like way too much work.

But Dr. Eastman smiles. "I love, love, love it."

We're so used to school administrators saying no, I don't think any of us expected this.

"Let me think," she says, sitting on Mr. Lu's desk. "We'll just need to hire custodians, right? If you can get enough staff and parent volunteers."

"We can do that," Mr. Lu says.

"I'll notify the police as a courtesy, but this is pretty straightforward, and it's going to be fabulous. I will also share that I am a huge thrifter. Pretty much everything my wife and I wear comes from this funky store I found in Greenwich Village in New York."

"Really?" Hannah says.

"Oh yeah. I should take y'all there on a field trip. They also do fabric recycling projects, where they create all kinds of things from fabric scrap collections."

I love, love, love this woman.

"I just had another idea," Hannah says. "What if we have a thrifted fashion show, like in the middle of the festival? We can get all different kinds of people to model."

The superintendent claps her hands. "I love it! Does that mean old folks like me? And Ms. Singh and Mr. Joe?"

"That would be great," Hannah says.

"Okay, then. You figure out the details, Lulu," Dr. Eastman tells Mr. Lu, "and email everything to me. I'll take care of the funding and the other stuff. I might need to journey down to the city for a fashion-show outfit. Our first festival together! It's going to be fabulous."

She blows us a kiss and clicks her ruby heels before leaving us all in shock that a superintendent could be that amazing.

"You can thank my old principal Ms. Milholland for her," Mr. Lu says. "She fought to get her hired."

"She calls you Lulu?" Elijah says to Mr. Lu.

"Hey, I told you we're BFFs."

FOUR WEEKS UNTIL FUNFEST CHECKLIST

- ☐ Invite composting company and set up compost tent (Shawn and Mary Kate)
- ☐ Organize electric-car show, invite dealers, and secure parking lot (Rabia and Elijah)
- ☐ Make anti-idling campaign posters (Rabia and Elijah)
- ☐ Come up with vegan recipes (Rebecca)
- ☐ Find facts about leaf blowers (Ben)
- ☐ Organize clothing swap and thrifted fashion show (Hannah and Jay)
- ☐ Plan refreshments, decorations, and entertainment (everyone)
- ☐ Recruit volunteers (everyone)
- ☐ Figure out marketing and publicity (everyone)
- ☐ Make the dance playlist (Lulu)

I have to plan a different kind of party, and I need help. I'm officially building a bat house for Lucy's thirteenth birthday.

Shawn has to be at the greenhouse after school, so I decide to ask everyone in climate class if they have time to help me with my birthday surprise for Lucy. The only one who doesn't have field hockey, soccer, community service club, or strings ensemble is Ben.

After all these weeks, I've barely talked to the kid, but I know he's a Boy Scout and he's made bat houses before.

It stopped raining, so we climb out the window and walk through the woods. It's a little awkward, but then I point out a patch of very unusual mushrooms, and as my sister always says, the ice is broken. We look for mushrooms the whole way to my house, where we pick up the supplies Dad left out for me: wood, a hammer, nails, and a pretty tall ladder.

"Do you like climate class so far?" I ask as we walk slowly down the sledding hill carrying the ladder.

"Yeah, how could you not like it?" Ben says. "I'm still bummed about that stupid grant money, though. If we had known, we could've left Shawn's name off the application. At least then we would have had a chance."

My stomach turns. "Wait, don't you think it would've been better if the mayor had understood that Shawn is part of this town?"

"Well, he's not exactly part of this town."

I don't want to fight with this kid, because I need him to help me with the bat house. But what he's saying is really upsetting to me.

"Can we rest for a second?" I say, setting down the ladder. "Ben, did you even hear the podcast? The mayor did not sound very nice at all. Can you at least admit that?"

"Can we please talk about mushrooms? I don't care about this stuff."

"Of course not. You're white. Why should you care?"

"Exactly."

I want that bat house, but I'm not going to stand here and listen to this.

"My head is kind of hurting," I say. "I think I need to do this a different day."

He shrugs. "I can build a bat house in my sleep because we did so many when I was in fifth grade. Do you want me to do it?"

"No, that's okay. You can leave the ladder here. I'll have my dad help me get it later."

He shrugs again and goes toward the woods.

"Hey, Ben?" I shout.

"Yeah?"

"I don't actually have a headache. I'm annoyed. Shawn was not treated right, and it bothers me that you don't care."

"I care about Shawn. I just don't care about the Apple-fest drama."

"Well, you should."

"Okay."

"Can you try to think of how Shawn must feel? Living in another place and going to school with all of us? Have you ever invited any of the kids from Hartford to a birthday party? Or to hang out? Because before this class, I never have."

"No. What are you even talking about?"

"I don't want to be mad, Ben. Can you maybe think about this on your way home?"

"Fine, Mary Kate. I'll think about it on my way home."

I don't know if Ben's actually going to think about it, but I'm glad I said something. Keeping it in would really make my head ache.

CLIMATE CLASS APPLICATION ESSAY

My name is Benjamin Haynes Lettle, and I am a Boy Scout and a seventh grader at Fisher Middle School. When I heard about this climate class, I knew I had to apply because I am on a mission to ban leaf blowers in Connecticut and I need more information for my case.

I started a lawn-care business two years ago to earn money for a trip to Montana I was signed up to take. My parents said I had to earn half of the money myself, so I started asking people if I could rake leaves for them. They all said, "No, thank you. We have leaf blowers."

My dad said he wanted me to earn money the old-fashioned way, plus it was good exercise, but I couldn't find anyone to pay me to rake. I looked up leaf blowers on Google to see if I could buy one and make money blowing leaves instead of raking. I was shocked to find out that leaf blowers are worse for the environment than pickup trucks. I read that using a leaf blower for an hour is the same as driving a car for a hundred miles. Plus, they are very irritating to people who hate loud noises going on all day. I decided to side with my dad and stick to raking.

I want to eliminate leaf blowers here in Connecticut, like people are doing in other places. That would improve the climate and my lawn-care business.

ON THE BUS

"Of course we'll help with the festival," Molly says. "Are you kidding, Mare? We've been waiting to do something with the Bearsville Climate Club."

"I was thinking you could design a movable mural," I say, "like something on wheels that has to do with environmental justice."

"Yes! We can totally do that," she says. "That way, after the festival, we can wheel it someplace else in town."

"Let's try to keep it a surprise for climate class. They'll love it."

Molly's texting everyone. She's smiling a lot, so she's probably also texting the sophomore, who actually has a real name, George.

I add a new intention and say it and my first intention in my head over and over again.

Charlotte Lane wins in a landslide.

The Bearsville Climate Club Fall Funfest is a huge success.

THIRD PERIOD

There's something wrong with Ms. Lane.

She's usually very excited about Poetry Friday, but right now she's staring at her phone and making a face like she just ate the school tuna roll.

"What's wrong with Ms. Lane?" Jay whispers.

"No idea," I say.

"Um. I, uh, we're going to move Poetry Friday to Monday, and right now I'll have you write the October letter to yourselves in class. How does that sound?" Her voice is abnormally high.

We all nod and fumble around for paper and pens.

I look back at Shawn. He shrugs.

OCTOBER LETTER TO MYSELF

Dear Mary Kate,

We're writing a letter to ourselves in class because there's obviously something wrong with Ms. Lane if she doesn't feel like teaching poetry. Maybe she's sick or has period cramps, or she forgot to pay a bill or something. Speaking of period cramps, I still haven't gotten my period. Sarah says that's normal and it will come back. Rebecca says all of her sisters and their mom get their periods the same week because that happens with women who live together. Mom doesn't get her period anymore. Maybe that's the problem.

Okay, now I'm really starting to worry about Charlotte. She's scrolling through her phone a mile a minute.

Mark and Sarah are both coming home this weekend. I asked Mark to help me build the bat house for Lucy's surprise. All I have to do is make him an apple crisp and sleep on the couch so he can sleep in my room, because he hates sleeping on the couch, and Dad and Mom turned his room into an office. I said fine,

*and now I'm having the whole climate class over on
Saturday to plan for the festival and the next podcasts,
so Mark better not be annoyed when we're all in his
band room.*

 *Bell is ringing. Charlotte didn't even say, "Have a
good weekend."*

Love,
Me

AT LUNCH

"Does the superintendent have a nickname for you, Mr. Beam?" I ask.

"Um. She pretty much likes to call me Beamer," he says. He's staring at his phone with a very stressed look on his face, which is forming two deep lines between his eyebrows.

"Hey, Beamer," I say. "Are you good at party planning, Beamer?"

"Enough with Beamer. I'm not a fancy car. But who do you think threw the staff cookout where we all got our nicknames?"

"Can you be on our festival planning committee?" I ask.

Mr. Beam barely looks up. "Yeah, I can do that. But I need to focus on something at the moment."

I can literally see he's on Facebook.

Mr. Beam told me when Ms. Santos-Skinner broke up with her boyfriend because he was cheating on her with a woman who worked at the Michaels craft store. He told me that Mr. Joe has hair implants. He told me that Mr. Parker has a shopping addiction. And that Mr. Dern is missing a big toe from a lawn-mower accident.

Okay, he didn't actually *tell* me all that, but he said it to other teachers loud enough for me to hear.

But right now, every time I ask him what's going on, he says, "It's not appropriate to share information about other staff members."

Mr. Lu collects our "Ten Examples of Really Cool Carbon Sinks" homework the second we get to class and then sends us out the window with a pop quiz he handwrote, then copied on his classroom printer.

"You never told us we had a quiz," Elijah says.

"That's why it's called a 'pop' quiz," Mr. Lu says. "Come on, out the window."

I sit on the bench under a tree with Rabia.

"What is going on?" Rabia asks. "Why are the teachers acting strange?"

"I don't know, but it's making me nervous," I say.

"It's making us all nervous," Rabia says.

THE FACEBOOK POST I FIND ON
MOM'S LAPTOP WHEN I GET HOME

Dear Residents of Honey Hill,

It has come to my attention that my opponent, Charlotte Lane, has shown her true colors. She is so desperate to win this race, she's using her students to film and distribute damaging videos with the goal of smearing me and my hardworking staff. I am disappointed and dismayed to find that this woman has stooped so low. We are conducting an internal investigation to see if campaign rules were violated when Charlotte Lane gave her eighth-grade students the task of creating a podcast in order to undermine my campaign. But in the meantime, I hope you'll think twice before voting for such an unprincipled person.

Thank you for your support during this difficult time for me and my family.

Mayor Brent Grimley

IN THE TREE HOUSE

Molly meets me in her tree house right away.

"I'm sick to my stomach," I say. "I feel like we've ruined Charlotte's chance to be mayor. I don't know if I've ever felt this way in my entire life." I slump over on the beanbag chair. I feel the tears busting out like hornets from a nest. I'm so sick of crying.

Molly stares at the mayor's Facebook post. She lets me cry in peace all over her beanbag chair while she furiously texts.

Within twenty minutes, I'm forced to meet George, the sophomore, with a red swollen face and snot bubbles coming out of my nose. Fortunately, he nods at me with a look on his face that says, *I get why you're crying.*

Navya and Bea follow him through the tree-house door, and they all sit at the tiny plastic table and look at the stupid Facebook post until Navya finally gives me a packet of tissues from the bottom of her backpack and Molly says, "We need to fix this."

THE REVENGE TIKTOK

"I'm Molly, and this is my tree house," Molly says. George moves the camera around to show the rest of us and all the old anti-dress-coding posters. "We live in a town where the mayor thinks it's cute to bring down his opponent by lying. We're here to set the record straight."

"Ms. Charlotte Lane did not have anything to do with Mayor Grimley's decision to kick the eighth-grade climate club out of the Applefest grant competition," Navya says. "She had nothing to do with us deciding to post a video of the mayor at Applefest. She had literally nothing to do with any of this."

"Mayor Grimley," Molly says, "maybe you should think about how to improve yourself and stop lying about Ms. Lane. We may not be able to vote, but we support Ms. Lane because she's a brilliant person and a great leader. And she doesn't lie."

Bea holds up sign that says MAYOR GRIMLEY IS LYING. George stops recording.

By the time I leave the tree house, there are already 970 views.

LETTER TO MY BABY NIECE ON HOW TO DEAL WITH STRESSFUL SITUATIONS

Dear Sweet Pea,

There will probably come a time when you have a very stressful situation happen and you don't know what to do. I highly recommend you go to your mom because she's so good at making stressful situations better.

Yesterday, the mayor of our town said some very upsetting things on Facebook. (I don't know if that will exist by the time you're twelve, but it's an irrelevant parent social media site.) He made it look like Charlotte was using my friends and me to get elected. I'm not going to get into the details, but it was all a lie.

My friends and I were so upset we didn't know what to do. But then your mom got here from Boston (with you), and she told me Charlotte felt horrible too and was furious that the mayor had lied and brought kids into the campaign. Charlotte said she doesn't want us helping with the campaign anymore because she wants to protect us. We felt like we failed her, but your mom told us and Charlotte to ignore the mayor's attack and keep doing what we're doing, especially since his Facebook post only got eight likes and it got forty-two angry faces.

I know that seems simple, but your mom is totally right. Let the mayor be petty and immature. We have work to do.

Your mom gave us her advice after we posted our tree-house TikTok, and she secretly admitted that the TikTok was pretty awesome.

Anyway, I have to go build a bat house with Uncle Mark.

> *Love,*
> *Auntie*

MY BROTHER, MARK

My brother, Mark, is mad that I messed up his band room, even though he moved out of the house before I was even born. But he says he forgives me because I took the time to make him the apple crisp and I'm using the room for a righteous cause, and he'll even get out his guitar and play for my climate club when they come over tonight. *Great. Another embarrassing family member.*

"Step it up, Pep," Mark says, blowing past me on his mountain bike with a sack of wood on his back. I don't know why Mark calls me Pep, but he has for as long as I can remember.

We get everything to the bottom of the sledding hill, and Mark sits down with his water bottle. "So, what's going on with you, Pep? Sarah says you're working on environmental stuff, huh?"

"We're trying. I'm in a climate-class pilot program at school, and we're organizing a zero-waste festival on Halloween weekend. That's why everyone's coming over, to work on planning."

"Good for you. I'm glad to see the movement is hitting the suburbs."

"How's Brooklyn?"

"It's fun. You need to come visit. I'll take you to all my vegetarian spots."

"That would be amazing."

Mark jumps up, grabs his bike, and runs it up the sledding hill. He speeds down so fast Mom would have a heart attack if she saw him.

"I needed to get that out of my system, and now we can work on the bat house," Mark says, walking toward the pole we carried down earlier. "Let's do this. Luce is going to love it."

It doesn't take long because Mark is really good at building things. I don't know why I was desperate to get help from Ben just because he's a Boy Scout. It would have taken us a week. Mark attaches the house to the pole, and we lift the pole into the hole we dug and secure it there. We step back and look at our finished project.

"It's perfect, Mark. Thank you for coming all the way up here to do this."

"Anything for you, Pep. When are you going to surprise Lucy?"

"Next weekend, on her actual birthday."

"You have to let me know her reaction."

"I will."

Mark packs all the tools on his back and takes off on his bike. I stand for a while, soaking in the cool morning air. It's still a little foggy at the far end of the preserve, and the mist over the hills is pretty next to the changing leaves. I take a minute to plan the final details of Lucy's surprise in my mind. Now I just have to make sure her mom keeps her away from the preserve for a week.

I walk home slowly, reciting the intentions I've gotten used to saying over and over again.

Charlotte Lane wins in a landslide.

The Bearsville Climate Club Fall Funfest is a huge success.

THE BEARSVILLE CLIMATE CLUB
MEETS THE MURPHYS

The whole climate class comes over to work on the festival. Shawn's sister, Sydney, also comes, and Jay brings Andrew Limski, whose parents wouldn't let him join our climate class, even though when we were in fifth grade, he sat in front of Town Hall by himself every Friday with a sign that said THERE IS NO PLANET B.

They're all talking about the tree-house TikTok, which is getting more views than any TikTok made by anyone else I know in real life.

"How could he be so mean to Ms. Lane?" Rabia says. "She's the nicest person."

"She's trying to make the town better. She doesn't deserve this," Hannah says.

I hope the people voting feel the same way.

It takes a while to get focused. First, Sarah comes up to the band room with Pea, and everyone wants to hold her. Then Mark comes up and starts telling stories about his old band days, and I have to kick him out, but not before the entertainment committee agrees to let him play his guitar at the festival.

"Should I play a few songs now to see if I'm a good fit for the vibe?" Mark asks.

"No, thanks. We trust you," I say, giving him a *Can you please leave? Because you're acting like Dad* look.

"Can we get something done before my mom comes?" Rebecca says. "We need to focus."

"The first rule of climate club should be: 'You're kicked out if you keep distracting people,'" Ben says.

"Then everyone here would be kicked out by now," I say.

Sydney says she's glad she's not in our grade, because we are really bad at focusing, and sixth graders could do this a lot better.

It takes getting shamed by a sixth grader for us to finally focus.

We email the Fisher staff to ask for volunteers.

We make a cool flyer.

We find people to lend tents and tables and other stuff.

We get our parents to ask for clothing racks and hangers on the community Facebook page.

We decide instead of a thrifted fashion show with a stage, we're going to do a parade around the front circle so we can have a lot of models and space for the audience.

We go through yes emails from electric-car dealers and even have a guy offer to teach a pop-up workshop about how electric cars work, *and* we find out DJ Dizzy Lu can plug his sound system into an electric car that has been charged off the grid.

We decide on pumpkins and hay bales and other fall decorations.

We confirm that the social-justice club will do online publicity for the festival. (In addition to the secret surprise.)

We come up with guests for podcasts and set the first interview up for tomorrow.

We agree to start researching zero-waste refreshment ideas.

"Take that, sixth graders," Shawn says, flicking Sydney.

And then we get tired and decide to eat candy and listen to Elijah's playlist while we search for costume ideas for the dance.

I get the urge to text Lucy. **We're planning the festival up in Mark's band room. Any chance you could come for a while?**

I expect her not to answer or to tell me how frustrating I am. But twenty minutes after I text, she shows up, with a giant bag of kettle corn. Elijah convinces me to go get my avocado costume, and he comes up the stairs in it, yelling, "Guacamole!"

Lucy laughs when the entire climate class practices runway walking, which turns into a dance party.

And for the first time in months, she stays.

We sleep squished together with our heads on opposite sides of the old couch in Mark's band room.

I think it's the best sleepover of my life.

CLIMATE CLASS APPLICATION ESSAY

ANDREW LIMSKI

When I was in fifth grade, I sat in front of Town Hall with a sign that said THERE IS NO PLANET B every Friday for twenty-two weeks after I saw Greta Thunberg giving a speech about how we all need to do something about the climate crisis. The only thing I could think to do in fifth grade was sit with a sign like Greta.

I don't know if I changed any minds, but I realized if I really wanted to do something, I should start by convincing my parents to switch all our light bulbs to LEDs, which they finally did after I kept hanging my THERE IS NO PLANET B sign on the refrigerator and the bathroom mirror and other places. I told them if they switched to LED lights, I wouldn't bother them anymore with the sign.

When I stopped going to Town Hall, they thought that meant I wouldn't talk about the climate crisis anymore. But I'm not stopping that until they actually listen. I feel like I know a lot about the climate crisis, but I want to take this class because I need help getting people to actually listen.

My parents think my obsession with the climate crisis is causing too much anxiety. I keep trying to tell them that THEY are causing my anxiety because they won't take this seriously.

THE BEARSVILLE CLIMATE CLUB PODCAST

ME: My name is Mary Kate Murphy, and this is *The Bears-ville Climate Club Podcast.* I'm on the phone with Jay Mendes and his neighbor, Zoe Zhang, a senior at Honey Hill High School. Jay, can you tell us about today's topic?

JAY: Yes. I thought it would be a good idea to invite Zo to talk about her "no new clothes" senior project. Can you tell us about it, Zo?

ZOE: Yes. Thank you for having me. I did a lot of research on fast fashion and how much more clothing we buy than people bought fifty years ago. I looked at my closet and realized how many things I bought just because shopping was a fun activity, not because I needed clothes. So I decided to make fast fashion my senior project topic.

JAY: What are you doing for the project?

ZOE: I'm making a video that explains where our clothing comes from and how it's possible to scale down our wardrobes and only wear a few pieces. It's not about buying a ton of clothes at the thrift shop. It's about buying fewer items and wearing them more.

JAY: That makes sense.

ZOE: Then I decided to make a pledge. I will not buy a

single new item of clothing my entire senior year. If I need something, I'll borrow it.

JAY: How's that going so far?

ZOE: It's only the beginning of the year, but I didn't go back-to-school shopping. It was a little sad to break that tradition of going to the outlets with my mom and my sister, but I'm getting more creative with the clothes I have and it's actually fun. I have so many people from last year's senior class already offering their formal dresses if I need them.

JAY: I could definitely go a whole year without shopping for clothes. I don't like shopping.

ZOE: I love it, but I love our planet more. By the way, you really opened my eyes about hemp clothing. The last thing I bought, back in July, was a hemp sweatshirt. It's so soft. I wear it all the time.

JAY: Thanks. I recommend you all look into hemp clothing. It's softer and better for the earth than cotton. So, Zo, is your message to listeners to try the pledge and see if they can do it too?

ZOE: Yes. I think you'll be surprised. It's not as hard as it sounds.

JAY: Thanks, Zo. And good luck with your project.

ZOE: Thank you, Jay and Mary Kate and the Bearsville Climate Club.

ME: That was a great conversation. To learn more about fast fashion and ways to cut back on shopping, save the date for our Bearsville Climate Club Fall Funfest, on Saturday, October thirtieth, from one to four p.m.

ON THE BUS

It's cold and rainy and eerily dark for three in the afternoon. I sit in the front of the bus with Talia and Molly and take out my phone to see how many views the tree-house TikTok has gotten since yesterday.

I have a bunch of texts from Lucy. All of them say: **Check your email.**

There are two emails in my inbox, and I've been waiting for both of them.

The first one is Lucy's lab results from Dr. H. I don't really understand them, but Lucy has written a message at the top of the page: *I don't have one tick-borne illness. I have FOUR tick-borne illnesses. Positive for Lyme disease. Positive for bartonella. Positive for babesiosis. Positive for ehrlichiosis.*

> **LUCY:** Did you check your email?

> **ME:** Yeah. That's a lot of diseases for a tiny tick.

> **LUCY:** Dr. H is giving me another medicine, and he says I'm going to get better.

> **ME:** I know you will.

LUCY: We all want to see Shawn
Hill and his mom. We need to
thank them.

I show Molly the email, and we Google all the long names of the tick-borne illnesses.

They are common in Connecticut. They are carried by deer ticks, which are much smaller than other ticks. They can be treated with antibiotics, but sometimes require months of treatment. They are getting worse because of warmer winters due to climate change.

"Climate change," I say.

"This is so disturbing," Molly says.

I feel itchy thinking about the number of creepy ticks we've pulled off Claudia and Murphy.

Molly keeps reading. "This can be really serious."

"Like, how bad?"

"Don't read it, Mare. She's taking medicine. She's going to be fine."

When we get off the bus, Molly stops me. "Are you okay?"

I nod. "I'm glad she finally got an answer after all those doctors."

"Need a Molly hug?" Molly is a very good hugger.

I nod again.

We hug awkwardly because our backpacks are on our backs. Molly smells like lavender oil. The rain soaks our heads.

"She's going to be fine," Molly says again.

My body collapses a little, like she's squeezing months of anxiety out of me. "I've been really worried about her."

"I know."

I don't want to cry again. I cried the last time I was with Molly. I think I've cried more in a month than in my entire past twelve years put together. But I have no control over it. First come the tears, then the snot bubbles. Molly digs around in the front pocket of her backpack and hands me a pair of blue flowered underwear to blow my nose.

"Ew. No."

"They've never been worn. They're my backups."

I blow my nose on the underwear and stand there in the downpour, feeling relieved and emotional all at the same time. Holding in a cry can be like holding in pee. Eventually, you're going to soak some underwear in the middle of the street.

"You okay, girls?" Mrs. Caldwell calls out from a bedroom window.

"Yes, we're okay," Molly says.

"This too shall pass," Mrs. Caldwell yells. "Whatever it is."

"How does she know?" I whisper.

"Nosy people know everything."

I say goodbye to Molly and walk through the muddy patch of grass toward my driveway. I start to say my intentions, and then I realize I'm missing the most important intention of all.

Charlotte Lane wins in a landslide.

The Bearsville Climate Club Fall Funfest is a huge success.

Lucy is all better.

Dear Ms. Murphy,

Thank you for your letter of concern in regard to your notice of disqualification from the Applefest grant competition. While I understand your disappointment and realize this is difficult for young people such as yourselves to accept, we were simply following Regulatory Code #7543, which states that applicants must be residents of the town. To change that rule would complicate our grant process and potentially open up our community to any number of unwanted outside influences.

We are not responsible for whether teachers receive messages.

And I must tell you I take great offense to your accusations of racism. I'd like to share a personal story with you. My good friend Lieutenant Charles P. Smith served his nation and his community and was a loving father and grandfather. I was one of the golf club members who voted in favor of admitting him to the club. We spent hundreds of hours on the golf course together and at club barbecues with our families.

We lost Charles nearly a year ago, and I miss him dearly.

And Charles, who happened to be an African American, would be appalled to read your shameful letter.

I recommend you choose your words more wisely.

Sincerely,
Mayor Brent Grimley

MOLLY'S RESPONSE TO THE MAYOR'S EMAIL

ME: He's missing the point.

MOLLY: I cannot believe he played the "I have a Black friend" card.

ME: He HAD a Black friend. He also used his friend who passed away to try and prove he's not a racist, which is not being a very good friend.

MOLLY: The guy is clueless. I will seriously recruit as many people as I can to help Ms. Lane win.

ME: What should I do about this letter?

MOLLY: Show everyone?

ME: Already done.

WHY DO ALL OUR FIGHTS HAPPEN ON FETTUCINE NIGHT?

Mark and Sarah are gone, and the house is quiet. It's just dog snores and Mom talking on the phone with Lucy's mom, while I do math homework at the kitchen counter.

"I'm so glad you finally have answers."

"I know. She's an angel."

"Yes, I think a gift basket is a great idea."

"Okay, say hello to Michelle and your mom."

"Will do."

She hangs up the phone and calls Dad in for dinner.

"I know Lucy shared the test results with you," she says, spooning spinach fettucine with pesto sauce into bowls. "Her whole family is grateful for your help. You fought to get Lucy to Dr. H."

"It was really Shawn and his mom," I say.

"Oh, heck yes. Lucy's family is going to send them a big basket."

When adults don't know how to show gratitude, they send gift baskets.

Dad comes in from puttering (his word, not mine) around the garage and washes his hands. He takes the rolls out of the oven and the salad out of the fridge and sets them on the table.

"What's the scoop?" he says, like he does practically every night at dinner.

I soak my roll in pesto sauce. "There's actually a lot of scoop."

Mom tells him about the tick-borne diseases and how Lucy is already starting to show signs of improvement, even after only a few weeks on the antibiotics.

"I read that Lyme disease is getting worse because of climate change," I say.

"Not surprised at all," Dad says. "With warmer winters, the little jerks aren't dying off. They're multiplying."

"We need to be super vigilant," Mom says. "Especially you, Mary Kate. You need to strip down and check yourself for ticks every time you go to the preserve. We don't want to mess around with this."

"I'll try."

"Problem is," Dad says, "you're going to play a frustrating game of tick or freckle."

I listen to bookstore talk and eat my fettucine and wonder if I should bring up the email that's been making me sick to my stomach for hours.

"I have something else going on that I haven't brought up," I say, "because I don't want to fight with you."

"We don't fight in our family, Mary Kate," Dad says. "We might disagree sometimes, but come on. We're not fighting folks."

I picture Sarah saying, "Because they refuse to deal with anything."

"What's on your mind?" Dad says.

Mom is squirming in her chair. She's probably wondering what uncomfortable topic Sarah has planted in my helpless twelve-year-old brain.

"Okay, I'm breaking the no-phones-at-the-table rule to read you something." I grab my phone from the counter and read the email I wrote to the mayor and then his response.

Mom stares at her fettucine like she's waiting for it to go airborne and strangle her. She finally swallows hard and breaks out her high-pitched voice. "Well, I'm not so sure it was a great idea to send something like that to the mayor. We own a business in town. I don't think we should be rocking the boat when it's not necessary."

"When it's not necessary? You mean when it doesn't affect you? Give me a break, Mom. I'm not sorry I sent that letter."

"Mary Kate, I don't want to frustrate you, but I see his point. Calling someone racist is a strong accusation. I mean, what would happen if they changed the rules for this grant and people flooded the town trying to get the money?"

"You sound exactly like the mayor. How are you even saying this right now?" *Hornets. Hornets. Hornets.* "You honestly think people are going to flood the town looking for money? These students spend most of their day five days a week here, and they're not even included as members of our community. Dad, can you please tell me you get this?"

"I see both sides. I absolutely see how he could be a little hurt and offended that his decision to stick to the rules was taken that way. But I do agree he could have made an exception to the rule in this case and let your climate club remain in the competition."

"We don't just need exceptions to rules. We need to

change the rules." I throw my fork into my half-eaten bowl of fettucine. I can't eat. The hornets have gnawed their way through my insides. "Can I be done?"

"Mary Kate, why on earth are you getting so worked up about this?" Mom says. "I'm not following your logic."

"Mom, I know you're not following my logic. But I'm not following the fact that the two most educated people I know can be so clueless."

I get up, throw my napkin on the table, run upstairs, and text Sarah: **THE ARTICLES AREN'T WORKING.**

THE CLIMATE CLUB'S RESPONSE TO THE MAYOR'S EMAIL

HANNAH: He did have a good friend who was Black, so maybe he really was just focusing on the rules.

REBECCA: You can have a Black friend and still do racist things that you might not realize are racist. Ask my parents. And you heard what he said on that recording.

BEN: Can we stop talking about the grant and focus on climate change before the planet dies?

REBECCA: We can talk about racism and climate change at the same time, Ben.

BEN: Well, climate change is a much bigger problem. It's life or death, okay?

JAY: So is racism, bro.

MY TEXT TO SHAWN

ME: You okay?

SHAWN: Yeah. I don't feel like talking. I'm really, really tired.

ME: I understand.

I realize it's not fair to tell my parents to read the books on their Black Lives Matter display table without reading the book Mr. Beam gave me about environmental justice, which has been sitting at the bottom of my backpack. I stay up until 2:00 a.m. on a school night reading about how connected climate change is to racial and economic inequality.

I'm twelve, and I understand this. I feel like I should write a book report for my parents, the mayor, and half the people in my climate club.

ON THE BUS

Will brings up something the rest of us hadn't even thought of. "Has anyone noticed the mayor belongs to the golf club that won the grant money? Don't you wonder if anyone watched him count the votes?"

"Whoa," Molly says. "That is true."

"I don't think there's any way to know," I say. "But nothing this guy does would surprise me."

I rush down to Ms. Lane's room before anyone gets there, show her the email, and bring up the thing about the golf club.

"Mr. Lu shared the email," she says. "And Sarah and I thought of the golf club thing too."

"Mr. Lu saw the email?"

"He's on your climate-club group chat."

I think we'd all forgotten our teacher is on that chat. Otherwise, it wouldn't be full of not-teacher-friendly language. I make a note to myself to start a new group chat right away.

"It really bothers me," I tell Ms. Lane. "I mean the mayor stuff."

"It really bothers me too," she says. "But I need you to focus on your argumentative essay today and save political stuff for out of school, okay?"

I hope she doesn't get mad at me, but I write my argumentative essay on why Charlotte Lane should be mayor of Honey Hill.

Mr. Beam is sitting at a table stacked with books.

"Look what I got you, Murphy," he says, smiling.

"Wow. My librarian got me books," I say. "I thought we agreed to small talk and Twitter."

"Oh, these aren't any old books. They're a whole lot of climate-change books, including fast-fashion books and electric-vehicle books and composting books. I was thinking, what if we open up the back door of the library for the festival and build a cozy book lounge, and people can browse, and take out books, and maybe make trash-to-treasure bookmarks or something?"

"Now I know why you win so many librarian awards."

"I actually win those because of my wit and charm."

I stop at the bathroom on my way to Spanish to do my usual period-paranoia check, and Rabia's standing in front of the mirror, wiping her face with a wet paper towel.

"Are you okay?" I ask. She's obviously been crying.

"Yeah, just friend stuff."

"What happened?"

"Do you ever feel like nobody understands? Like we're the only ones who care about the planet?"

"Yeah, I've been feeling like that my whole life."

"All Alli and Aarya want to do is look at TikTok, talk about soccer and boys, and take pictures of themselves. And I get it. I really do. But honestly, I feel like I'd rather hang out with a kid who wears bow ties and watches videos on carbon capture than my own best friends."

"Elijah?"

"Yes. Weirdly, Elijah." She laughs and blows her nose. "Now they don't want to go to the Halloween dance. They want to go to some kid's house because his parents won't be home that night, which they know I won't be allowed to do anyway. And they're whispering about all their plans and ignoring me. It's so frustrating. It makes me feel empty inside."

"I'm really sorry, Rabia. All I can say is I know that feeling. I don't really talk about it, but I'm constantly worried about Lucy."

"I'm so sorry she's sick."

"It's okay. She's starting to feel better. I just understand what you're feeling."

"I'm glad we have climate club," Rabia says.

"Me too. And you can come to the dance with me if you want. I'd love it."

"Really? That would be great."

EIGHTH PERIOD

Mr. Lu collects our "Modern Fossil-Fuel Barons Who Are Messing Up the Planet" homework and waves us over to the rug, and we sit kindergarten-style.

"We need to address the elephant in the room," he says. I assume he's going to say something goofy, but his face is serious, and he sits down and clears his throat. "We need to talk about racism and climate change. I know this is eighth-grade science and not a college-level sociology class. But here's the thing: wealthy communities have a history of pushing polluters and huge honking things like incinerators out of their towns and into lower-income places that often have a disproportionate number of Black and brown families. And why do a higher number of people of color live in these areas?"

Nobody raises a hand, because I don't think any of us really know.

"Because of something called redlining, where banks refuse to give loans and real estate companies refuse to sell homes to people of color in places like Honey Hill. We may not have had official segregation like other states, but there are all kinds of laws and rules in communities like ours that are intended to keep out entire groups of people. Does this make sense?"

We nod.

"So when a town refuses to think about how to bring equity into laws, rules, and, yes, Applefest grant competitions, they are, in my opinion, enforcing a system of racism. Do you understand?"

"Kind of?" Ben says.

"Let's put it this way," Mr Lu says. "If the town council asked themselves, 'Is this law inclusive? Does it make it easier for families of every race and ethnicity to feel part of our town?' every time they made a rule or a law, then maybe the grant rules would have allowed for our class to participate."

"But Elijah is Black too," Hannah says. "I just don't get how the rule is racist."

Everybody looks at Elijah.

"Just because Elijah is Black and happens to live in town doesn't mean rules and laws aren't in place to make it harder for people of color to feel welcome or included," Mr. Lu says.

"I've lived here my whole life, and half the time even I don't feel welcome or included," Elijah says. "Like the time Kyle Rudolph's dad followed me around the lacrosse store after I literally heard the store owner whisper to him that I looked suspicious. I was like, 'Dude, I played lacrosse with Kyle for three years.'"

"Oh, man," Mr. Lu says. "I'm so, so sorry he did that to you, Elijah."

"Do you want me to keep going?" Elijah asks. "Because I have a lot of stories."

"You can if you want to share," Mr. Lu says.

"I could tell stories all day, but most of them involve

people in our town calling me the n-word, so . . . But, yeah, Shawn and I always joke about how teachers mix us up all the time. I mean, there are only a few Black kids in the whole school. You'd think they'd have a harder time keeping the white kids straight." Elijah shakes his head. "I know Shawn and I aren't the only ones. Rabia gets mean comments for wearing the hijab. Jay gets it for being Puerto Rican. You probably get it too, being a Chinese guy."

Ben shakes his head. "I had no idea all that stuff happens."

"Yeah, it happens," Shawn says.

Hannah is literally crying. "I'm so sorry. This is so upsetting. What can we do to be better friends?"

Not cry and make it about you, I think, *when they're trying to share difficult stories maybe?*

"I guess if you see it," Elijah says, "don't just sit there and pretend it's not happening."

"And let me change the subject when I feel like changing the subject without making a big deal out of everything?" Shawn says.

"Fair ask," Mr. Lu says.

"I'm trying to start a climate club in Hartford, and I need a lot of help."

Mr. Lu gives him an elbow bump. "Then we shall help you. Who wants to jump in on this with Shawn?"

Every single one of us raises our hands.

BAT MITZVAH DAY

It's Lucy's thirteenth birthday. It's also her bat mitzvah day—or it would have been if her parents hadn't canceled everything.

I'm nervous she's not going to feel good today or that she won't like my surprise. I call her the second I wake up.

"Happy birthday, Luce!" I say. "I know it was supposed to be your bat mitzvah day, and that didn't happen, and I wanted to plan something to cheer you up. Do you feel okay enough to go to the preserve tonight?"

"I don't care how sick I feel," Lucy says. "I'm going."

"I'll be at your house for cake. My surprise is after."

"I'll rest until then."

"Okay. Good idea. I can't believe you're a teenager."

"You're next."

I thought about inviting Lucy's friends from the basketball team, or Molly and her friends, or people from climate club, but I wasn't sure how she would feel or if she could even make it tonight. So I decided it would just be the two of us. And the bats, and the fairies, and cake leftovers, and sparkling cider, and the moon.

LETTER TO MY BABY NIECE
ON HER GRANDPARENTS

Dear Sweet Pea,

I'm currently barely speaking to your grandparents. This is because I feel like even though they are surrounded by books, there are some things they don't want to think about. Or maybe they don't have to think about things like racism and climate change, so they just don't care.

I'm not saying they're bad people. They are great, actually. They're always home if I need them. They cook really good food. They both play piano, and they love to sit on the screened porch and listen to the birds. But when I'm having a real problem, or I'm trying to understand something that's bad in the world, they just want to put on classical music and hide in the garden.

I shouldn't complain to you, because they're your grandparents and they love you. They love all of us. I hope when you're twelve, they've gotten better so you don't have to be as frustrated as I am sometimes.

Love,
Auntie

BAT MITZVAH NIGHT

When I get to Lucy's, her aunt Michelle and her grandma and her other aunt, Barb, and her favorite little cousins and her grandparents from her dad's side are all there.

All Lucy wanted for her birthday was Thai food, cake, and for everyone not to get mad when she goes to the preserve with me. They're just happy she's willing to eat something without freaking out that her food might be contaminated.

"Hey, Mary Kate," the other grandma says. "We're so happy Lucy has you in her life."

"Thanks," I say. I'm not sure how else to answer that.

Everybody makes small talk, which Lucy and I are both bad at, and I keep looking at my phone.

"Let's go," she whispers after her family is sitting in the living room, having coffee and making more small talk.

We go out the back door and through the fairy woods to the clearing. I tell her she has to close her eyes, and I lead her slowly to the edge of the pond.

"Okay, Luce. Happy *bat*, as in flying creature, mitzvah!"

She opens her eyes, and I point up at the bat house.

"You made me a bat house? I can't believe it." She stands and stares for a long time. "I'm so happy right now."

"Come on, there's more," I say, leading her to the blanket I set up under the weeping willow, where I hung eighteen felt bats—because eighteen is a lucky number for Jewish people—and solar-powered twinkle lights, which are already twinkling in the October dusk.

We pile on blankets, and drink warm sparkling cider from the thermos, and watch the bat house. I look through the binoculars and think of how much Shawn would love this. I send him a picture of Lucy smiling up at the bat house, and then I forward it to Mark.

Nice, Pep! Mark texts.

Just as the colors are fading across the early night sky, a bat streaks by, and then another.

"Do you think they'll notice the house?" I ask.

"Yeah, they'll notice. But right now, they're looking for dinner. Or breakfast, actually."

We eat leftover lemon cake and watch the bats dance against the tree silhouettes.

"Thank you for my bat mitzvah, Mary Kate," Lucy says. "It's the most amazing birthday gift I've ever had."

And because I'm her best friend and I know her better than anyone in the world, I know she means it.

"It's way better than my parents' so-called surprise," she says.

"I mean, a trip to Florida is also nice."

"It's not like we're staying in an eco-lodge."

"True."

I don't care that Lucy is thirteen, or that I'll be thirteen in twenty-seven days, and we're supposed to be too old for fairies. They are here. I feel them. They might be tiny, but their magic is more powerful than all that is and all that ever was.

TEATIME

When I get home, the only one in the kitchen is Claudia, who barks like a maniac and thinks I'm an intruder because I came from the preserve wearing a headlamp.

I knock on Mom and Dad's bedroom door. "I'm back."

They're both sitting up in bed, Mom with three pillows behind her and Dad with a backrest and a neck warmer. They're wearing the matching red flannel slippers that Sarah got them last Christmas. It's colder in the house than it is outside because Dad won't turn on the heat until after a frost, which is good for climate change but bad for my freezing bones.

"How was it?" Dad asks.

"Perfect. She really loved it," I say. "Do you want tea?"

"No, thanks," Mom says, pointing to the coaster and teacup on the bedside table.

She pats the bed like I'm an old dog who doesn't feel like climbing up, and Dad slides his glasses down his nose so he can see me. I'm starting to wonder what is happening here.

"Can you just say whatever you're going to say? You're making me nervous."

"It's nothing bad, Mary Kate. It's just that Dad and I have been doing a lot of reading." She holds up a book. "And we spent a couple hours on a video chat with Sarah and Jason tonight because we wanted to be able to digest what we've read."

"We don't want to be clueless old white people," Dad says.

"Okay, and . . . ?"

"We'd like to say we're sorry for not being better at this and for thinking we were not racist when we should have been actively anti-racist."

I want to laugh at how awkward my parents are being, but it's obvious they're trying.

"Dad and I want you to know that we will keep working at this and we'll encourage our customers to give these books a try."

"And we're thinking about organizing a Clueless Old White People Community Read," Dad says.

"You should call it that," I say.

"We just need to choose the right book," he says.

"Hold on," I say. I run into my room and get the environmental-justice book Mr. Beam gave me. "Try this."

Mom takes it. "It'll be next on my pile. Can you write a summary for the store?"

"Sure," I say.

I leave them with their book stacks and tea and slippers, and our two old dogs snoring between them, and I text Sarah: **What did you do to my parents?**

She texts back: **Articles. Lots and lots of articles. And pretty soon I'm going to take out the big guns and make them watch a documentary.**

MIDNIGHT FACETIME WITH SHAWN

ME: Why are you still up?

SHAWN: Why are you?

ME: Lucy's bat mitzvah.

SHAWN: How was it?

ME: Perfect. Binoculars, bats, and cake. What are you eating?

SHAWN: Peanut butter on crackers. I don't know how to start this club in my neighborhood.

ME: Can't we put up flyers for a meeting and see if people show up?

SHAWN: What if nobody comes?

ME: My dad always says, "You won't know if you don't try."

SHAWN: My dad says that too. You'll go to the meeting?

ME: Of course.

SHAWN: I want to focus on composting first.

ME: Good idea. I gotta go. Now I want peanut butter.

THRIFTING

Mom and Molly and I go to Sarah's favorite thrift shop to look for clothes for the thrifted fashion parade. Hannah thought it would be a good idea to invite parents and grandparents to model too, so now Mom is in the parade, and we have to style her because she's never been seen out of the house in anything but beige pants, a floral turtleneck, and Teva sandals with socks.

The thrift shop smells like Mark's band room and scented candle.

Molly pulls out a dress from the 1970s, with big orange shapes that look like fish on it.

"That reminds me of the good old days," Mom says. "I'll wear that."

"Um, no. How about this?" I say, holding up a black turtleneck dress. "It's even a turtleneck, Mom."

"Yeah, that's more my style."

"You could wear these vintage boots with it," Molly says, "and a funky necklace or a brooch."

"I can't wear someone else's boots," Mom says. "That's yucky."

"Mom, if we're going to stop filling landfills with discarded clothing, we need to get over that. You really think foot germs last forty years? These boots are fine."

She takes the boots. And the dress. And a turquoise brooch shaped like a spider that I'm definitely going to steal.

"Who's that for?" I ask, pointing at the brown shirt with a pointy collar that Molly's buying.

"Oh, it's for George."

"Is he boyfriend George now?"

"I think he's boyfriend George. But I have no idea how that happens. Like, do you actually say 'Are you my boyfriend?' or is it automatic? And then when does the kissing happen? I don't know, Mary Kate. It's very confusing, and nobody seems to know."

"Obviously, I can't help you. Do you want me to ask Sarah?"

"Not yet. Let me try to figure it out."

Molly and I take pictures of the displays for the clothing swap, and the cashier tells us she knows a guy who will definitely lend us clothing racks for Halloween weekend if we advertise for him on social media.

I text Hannah, because Hannah likes being the boss. She texts: **YES.**

The cashier calls the guy. We make the deal. We have our clothing racks.

Mom drops us at home and wears the spider brooch on her regular turtleneck, for good luck, as she leaves to knock on doors for Charlotte.

One thing Mom and I agree on is that spiders definitely bring good luck.

I spend the rest of the day cleaning out my closet for the swap and reciting my growing list of intentions.

Charlotte Lane wins in a landslide.

The Bearsville Climate Club Fall Funfest is a huge success.

Lucy is all better.

People show up at Shawn's meeting.

AT LUNCH

Shawn and I are sitting with Mr. Beam, complaining about our Bs on Ms. Lane's argumentative essay assignment.

"I thought mine was so good," Shawn says.

"I wrote mine about her," I say.

"You really think she'd give you brownie points for that, Murphy?" Mr. Beam says. "It looks like you both forgot to look at the rubric."

"I despise rubrics," I say.

"Same," Shawn says.

"I have a meeting in seven minutes. What do you need from me?" Mr. Beam asks.

"We need help with refreshments for the festival and the dance," I say.

"I can't believe I'm offering this," Mr. Beam says, "but I could do a quick-bread bar with a big punch bowl of fresh cider from my friend Rick's farm."

"Really?" I say. "That would be perfect. What's quick bread?"

"You know, banana bread, pumpkin bread, apple bread—a rectangular-shaped cake without frosting? You slice it, and it's easy to pick up."

"Yeah, I love that stuff," Shawn says.

"Okay," Mr. Beam says. "I'll start baking and freezing."

"What if you made a few loaves for the climate-club meeting I'm trying to have in my neighborhood?" Shawn says.

He stares at Shawn. "I'll do it. But I choose the flavors."

"Deal."

Before class, we go down to the cafeteria with an idea and our fingers crossed.

Sue is cleaning up a puddle of spilled milk.

"Hey, kiddos," she says. "I'm trying not to cry. Get it?"

We stare at her blankly.

" 'Don't cry over spilled milk'?"

"Oh, I get it," I say.

We watch her mop.

"Do you need something?"

I look at Shawn.

"Yes," he says. "We had an idea. Our climate club is having a festival the Saturday before Halloween, and we were wondering if our classmate could use the cafeteria kitchen for demonstrations. Like, people will come watch her cook, and then we would have samples for people to eat as the refreshments for the festival."

"I love that idea," Sue says. "That's so cool."

"Really?" I say.

"Yes. You can absolutely use the kitchen. That's what it's here for, to feed people. I trust you to leave it the way you find it."

"You do?" Shawn says.

"Yeah, it's a kitchen, not a kitten. It's pretty resilient. Do whatever you want."

It's like our new superintendent is infecting everyone with yeses.

"Thank you," Shawn says.

We can't wait to tell Rebecca she's going to be making vegetarian food for everyone.

THE BEARSVILLE CLIMATE CLUB FALL FUNFEST

SATURDAY, OCTOBER 30
1-4 P.M.
FISHER MIDDLE SCHOOL

ELECTRIC VEHICLE SHOW

THRIFTED FASHION PARADE

COMPOST BOOTH

CLOTHING SWAP

ZERO-WASTE VEGAN COOKING
DEMONSTRATION

ENTERTAINMENT

AND SO MUCH MORE!

SUGGESTED DONATION: $10. PROCEEDS WILL GO TO A
COMPOSTING PROGRAM AT FISHER MIDDLE SCHOOL.

EIGHTH PERIOD

We have less than two weeks until the festival, and everyone is getting irritable. Hannah wants to control the fashion parade, but she only wants to work on styling; she doesn't want to do the boring stuff. But then she gets mad at Jay for doing the boring stuff wrong. Mr. Lu feels like we took on too much by also planning a dance the night of the festival, but we want to have something fun to look forward to after all this work.

"You told us the first rule of climate club is: 'Climate activism should be fun,'" Elijah says.

"When did I say that?"

"I don't know. Maybe I dreamed it," Elijah says.

"Isn't the festival fun enough?"

"No," we all say.

Mrs. Tucker comes in to give Mr. Lu a note, and we convince her to chaperone the dance with Ms. Santos-Skinner and Mr. Beam.

Everyone starts arguing about who's doing the most work, and who isn't doing enough, and who's in charge of the seventh-grade volunteers, because they need to be managed. Mr. Lu puts his gas mask on and crawls out the window.

Just when I'm about to scream at the top of my lungs,

"Can we go back to normal science class and take turns reading the textbook aloud and answering questions at the back of the chapter, like in Mrs. Fink's class?" Shawn jumps out of his chair and holds up his phone.

"I got two people signed up for my climate club, and we haven't even hung the flyers yet."

BATTERIES INCLUDED

I go with Rabia and Elijah to the car dealer after school to talk about the electric-car show.

We sit on the curb and wait for the car-dealer guy.

"I want that one right there," Elijah says, pointing at a dark-blue electric truck. "I heard you can run your whole house on that thing if the power goes out."

"That's so amazing," Rabia says. "I'm applying for an engineering camp this summer that focuses on designing new technologies for cars and other machines that don't use fossil fuels."

"Why didn't you tell me about that?" Elijah says.

"I don't know. I can get you an application."

"That sounds really hard," I say.

"Yeah, but they make it fun," Rabia says. "I'm obsessed with batteries. Like, you would totally make fun of me if you saw the experiments I do at home with my brother."

"Oh, I'm so coming over to your house," Elijah says. "Nobody in my entire family cares about batteries."

I never even knew caring about batteries was a thing.

The car dealer takes Rabia and Elijah into his office, and I wander around taking pictures of cars while they talk for forty-five minutes about batteries.

Then they finally choose the cars for the car show.

After we're done, I text Shawn a picture of the three of them with their heads under the hood of a truck. **I found something more boring than math drills. I might be late to meet you.**

He texts back: **Change of subject. My dad is coming home right before Thanksgiving. I'm so happy.**

I text him the hand-clapping and heart emojis.

The car-dealer guy invites us to choose whatever we want from the vending machine. He gives us his business card, which says **WAYNE CRESS, CERTIFIED EV SPECIALIST**, and we go back to the curb to wait for Rabia's mom to pick us up.

I eat my potato chips and listen to Rabia and Elijah talk about EV technology.

Rabia's mom pulls into the parking lot, and we get up.

"It's not electric," Rabia says. "Don't get me started."

I guess everyone's parents are annoying sometimes.

POLITICS

Rabia's mom drops me off at the bookstore to meet Mom, who isn't complaining (at least, not out loud) about driving me to Hartford this time. I'm helping Shawn and Sydney hang flyers around their neighborhood for Friday's meeting.

Mom already has a poster of the community read on the bulletin board, with my summary of the book Mr. Beam gave me.

> This book helps readers understand that communities of color, including Indigenous communities, are often the ones that are stuck with leaking pipelines, and factory pollution, and the old plumbing that never gets replaced and contaminates the water with lead, like in Flint, Michigan, and incinerator pollution going into their lungs and causing asthma, especially in children. Please read to learn how we can all be part of the solution, no matter where we live. (Written by M. K. Murphy, age 12.)

I almost ask Mom why she had to add that a twelve-year-old wrote the summary, but I see she's really trying, so I leave it alone.

Mom drops me at the greenhouse, and I walk through

Shawn's neighborhood to pass out flyers with Shawn and Sydney. They're both in a good mood because their dad is coming home. Sydney tells me she's saving money for boarding school because she's not in the mood to deal with Honey Hill anymore.

I don't ask her why she thinks boarding school will be different.

Most of the business owners let us hang the flyers, but one lady tells us she doesn't want to lose business because of political signs. We don't push it.

"How is protecting the planet political?" Sydney asks after we leave.

"Who knows?" I say.

It only takes us an hour to hang all the flyers.

Shawn already has four yes responses for his club.

"I'm tired," Sydney says. "Bye."

She walks toward home, leaving Shawn and me at the greenhouse.

"Did I hear her talking about boarding school?" Shawn asks.

"Yep," I say.

"I told you she was obsessed."

THE BEARSVILLE CLIMATE CLUB PODCAST

EPISODE FOUR

ME: My name is Mary Kate Murphy, and this is *The Bearsville Climate Club Podcast*. Today, we're broadcasting from a greenhouse in Hartford, Connecticut, where volunteers from the community grow food and deliver it to neighbors. Shawn Hill is here to tell you how that works and to make an exciting announcement. Hi, Shawn.

SHAWN: Thanks, Mary Kate. So, the greenhouse project came from a group of people, including my parents, who were fighting to get rid of the incinerator in Hartford. They realized how many neighborhoods in our city are what they call food deserts. People don't have access to grocery stores with fresh fruits and vegetables.

ME: Why is that?

SHAWN: Fresh food is expensive, and stores don't want to invest in poor communities, which means families in these communities have a harder time getting the food they need to be healthy. So we started growing our own food here. Now we grow and harvest greens and tomatoes all year long and deliver the fresh produce to neighbors. We even have a lady at a Caribbean restaurant up the block who bottles salad dressing for us.

ME: I've tasted it. It's delicious. Before we finish, can you tell us about your exciting announcement?

265

SHAWN: Well, now that we're closing the incinerator, we need to focus on reducing waste. One way to do it is by composting food scraps. I'm announcing that the first project of the new North End Climate Club will focus on composting and reducing waste as a climate-change solution.

ME: Is anyone welcome at the meeting?

SHAWN: We're inviting any kid up through high school. Please come to the North End Library on Friday, October twenty-second, at four p.m. And bring a friend.

ME: Thanks, Shawn. I'll see you there! And don't forget to join us at Fisher Middle School in Honey Hill for our Bearsville Climate Club Fall Funfest, Saturday, October thirtieth, from one to four. It's going to be . . .

ME AND SHAWN: Epic!

#INARELATIONSHIP

MOLLY: I think I just had what my
parents would call a date.

ME: How was it?

MOLLY: It was good. And we made
a plan to watch movies at George's
on the night of the festival.

ME: With Navya and Bea and
everyone, or just you two alone?

MOLLY: Just us alone.

ME: Well, okay, then.

MOLLY: Yep.

THE SHAWN-IS-REALLY-STARTING-A-CLIMATE-CLUB FLYER

**YOU'RE INVITED TO A MEETING
OF THE NEW STUDENT-RUN
NORTH END CLIMATE CLUB**

FRIDAY, OCTOBER 22
4 P.M.
NORTH END LIBRARY MEETING ROOM

ALL AGES WELCOME.
COME TALK ABOUT CLIMATE-CHANGE SOLUTIONS!

MY TEXTS WITH LUCY

LUCY: I don't feel nauseated!

        ME: What???

LUCY: Every single night I feel
nauseated for like three hours
before I go to bed, and the only
thing that makes it better is sleep.
I was trying to do the math packet,
and I looked at the time and
realized I'm NOT NAUSEATED!

        ME: This is possibly the best thing I
        ever heard!

LUCY: I'm going to that dance.

        ME: Definitely.

THE SANDWICH BOARD

I didn't know what sandwich boards were until last week, when Mom and Dad said we could advertise for the festival on a sandwich board in front of the bookstore. Sandwich boards sound much more delicious than they are. They're just two-sided signs.

We're on our way home from hanging flyers in Shawn's neighborhood when Mom stops at the red light in the middle of town, and there they are, about twenty people holding **REELECT GRIMLEY** signs. They're surrounding the old stuffed shirt himself, who's standing in front of a sandwich board that says **KEEPING HONEY HILL SAFE**.

"What is wrong with this guy?" I say.

I take a photo of the sandwich board and send it to Sarah.

SARAH: He's clearly implying Charlotte is going to let "unsafe" people into town, which is code for people who aren't white. Oh, and he dropped out of the debate.

ME: Why?

SARAH: We don't have a clue.

> **ME:** But she was going to bring up the Applefest grant.

SARAH: Exactly

"Can we throw an egg at him?" I ask Mom.

"No," she says.

"I can't vote," I say. "I should at least be able to throw an egg at the sandwich board."

Hornets are usually beneficial, gentle creatures. They mind their own business, and eat pests, and live their lives. Until you mess with their hive. Then they'll sting your face off.

Ms. Lane is the queen of our hive. She wants to make our community kinder and brighter for everyone who lives in Honey Hill. She would never try to scare people with a sandwich board. I feel my stinger twitching. I want to do something to help her win. But I'm twelve. And I have one friend trying really hard to get better so she can go to the dance. And another friend who just went on a "date." And another friend trying to plan a meeting for a club that people may or may not want to join. I'm kind of on my own.

I decide my "do something" is to respond to Mayor Grimley's email.

I give Mom some of the money Mrs. Caldwell gave me for dog-sitting back in August, to pay for a copy of the environmental-justice book and Sarah's favorite anti-racism book, and then I put the two books and a note that says *I hope you'll take time to read these important books* into a shoe box addressed to Mayor Grimley.

Dad promises to drop the box off at Town Hall.

WHEN LIFE GIVES YOU TICK-BORNE ILLNESSES

It's raining hard again, and Lucy's feeling pretty bad today. I'm up in her room, trying to help her organize a *portfolio*, which is a teacher word for *You've missed so much school you're never going to catch up, but we feel sorry for you, so you can do one big project and move on.*

"I'm okay," she says. She's sitting against a pile of pillows and making a gurgling sound in her throat. "I'm just feeling achy, like the rain is inside my bones. I think I'm going to do my portfolio on tick-borne illnesses and climate change so I can maybe help someone else someday."

"That's perfect, Luce."

We eat apples and cheese, and research all the microscopic creatures that live in ticks. Ticks are disgusting when they latch on to the skin and blow up like creepy raisins, but they are also kind of fascinating. I almost feel sorry for them. I wonder if they have aches and brain fog and mood swings from the diseases they carry too.

"You could do a comic book," I say. "Like, a day in the life of a sick tick."

"Oh my gosh, Mare. Would it be cheating if I steal that idea?"

"No. Mr. Lu said I could help you. This is going to be brilliant."

I only wish she hadn't seen the article on Lyme disease and heart damage.

"That's why you're taking medicine," I say.

"I know," she says. "I think I need to sleep a little."

We close the curtains and turn off the lights and get under the new fluffy white comforter Lucy got for her birthday. And we sleep, and sleep, and sleep. The rain pelting the roof makes me dream of waterfalls, and I wake up confused, with a bad stomachache. It's dark in the room, and my pillow is covered in drool. I hear Mom's voice in my head saying, *Too much cheese causes constipation. You'll get a stomachache.*

I think I had too much cheese. I decide I'm finally going to go vegan.

"You okay?" I say to Lucy. She's sitting up, rubbing her face with both hands.

"Yeah. Just groggy."

"That was a bizarre nap," I say, getting up to pee in Lucy's bathroom.

I sit on the toilet, and there it is. The no-show period I haven't had since July. I can't really move. The cramps are hurting me so much. I wait on the toilet while Lucy gets me a pad and some medicine and tea with ginger. She hands me new underwear and sweatpants.

"It had to be before the busiest week of my life," I say, before hobbling down the stairs and out to Dad's car. I get in and hunch over in the seat.

"What's wrong?" Dad asks.

I'm not in the mood to tell him I'm having three months of periods in one day. "I think I might be constipated."

"Did you have too much cheese?"

I close my eyes and wait for the medicine to kick in.

THE DEBATE

Sarah calls to tell us the mayor's office still hasn't said why he's dropping out of the debate. They just said the mayor will no longer be able to attend the debate they scheduled because he has an "unavoidable conflict." Ms. Lane offered to move around her schedule and debate him anytime, anyplace, but he "can't possibly find an open time."

Now everyone is calling him Mayor McChicken.

I'm sticking with Stuffed Shirt, because I like chickens.

THIRD PERIOD

Rebecca and I have been passing a marble notebook back and forth in English class, mostly writing about festival stuff, but sometimes about boys we would watch movies with on Halloween night.

Nobody from climate class, Rebecca writes.

I look around. There's one. Possibly.

Maybe Jay? I write.

Too soccer-ish, she writes back.

Ms. Lane is teaching us about the original people who lived on our land, the Tunxis Indians, and how important the river was for them. She wants us to write river poems.

Since Stuffed Shirt is too scared to debate Ms. Lane, I write, *we should try to get her to do a podcast and ask her some good questions.* I pass the notebook to Rebecca.

She might not want to do that because of what he said about her using her students.

True.

Ms. Lane grabs the notebook. "Seriously, girls?" She looks at us. "Not happening."

"How about Bearsville Climate Club questions?" I say, giving her the pout lip.

"I'll think about it. Poems. River. Focus."

Mr. Lu writes *NINE DAYS* on the smartboard. He tells us to hustle, then decides to talk about our Halloween costumes for fifteen minutes.

"I'm going as a compost heap," Shawn says. "I can pin food scraps on myself."

"Would it be copying if I do that too?" I say.

"No. I don't care. We can be twin compost heaps."

Half the class is going in their Applefest fruit and vegetable costumes.

Then Mr. Lu gives us a lesson on incinerators and why old incinerators that burn trash like the one near Shawn's neighborhood are so bad.

"They're finally getting rid of the incinerator," Shawn says, "but until they figure out what to do with the trash, they're just going to ship it to some other neighborhood that has a lot of poor people."

"That's why composting is so important," Mr. Lu says.

"Yeah, exactly," Shawn says. "Can you all help me present at the meeting tomorrow so it doesn't look like it's only me trying to organize this thing?"

We write out our presentation on scrap paper and practice taking turns.

"I really hope people show up for this," I say to Elijah, who's helping me take down our why-I-want-to-get-into-climate-class application essays after school so we can make a bulletin-board display about the festival.

"Me too," Elijah says.

FISHER MIDDLE SCHOOL
HALLOWEEN DANCE
FEATURING DJ DIZZY LU

SATURDAY, OCTOBER 30
7–10 P.M.
SCHOOL CAFETERIA

$5 SUGGESTED DONATION TO BENEFIT
THE BEARSVILLE CLIMATE CLUB

PLEASE WEAR A SECONDHAND, THRIFTED,
OR REPURPOSED COSTUME

BYO WATER BOTTLE
SNACKS PROVIDED BY THE FMS LIBRARY DEPARTMENT

LETTER TO MY BABY NIECE
ON GOOD DAYS AND BAD DAYS

Dear Sweet Pea,

This letter is to remind you that when you are having a lot of bad days, try to remember there will be good days ahead. It always happens that way.

Today was a good day. It started when the whole Bearsville Climate Club, even Andrew Limksi, showed up at the library in Shawn's neighborhood for the first meeting of the North End Climate Club. Mr. Lu even skipped his graduate school class to go, after he made us promise we wouldn't skip classes and say, "Mr. Lu does it." And Mr. Beam brought a giant tray of chocolate-chip quick bread.

We had decided in the car that if nobody showed up, we would take Shawn out for Italian ice and make a plan B, but we realized we were only worried because Shawn was worried. Actually, a bunch of people showed up, like at least twelve or thirteen, which is a lot for anything that has to do with climate change. (Sad but true.) And then Shawn's mom came with another group of kids, from the school where she's a social worker. Most of the people were around our age, a couple were older, and there was an adorable

281

eight-year-old who reminded me of Andrew back when he was sitting in front of Town Hall every week in fifth grade.

Shawn gave a really good speech about the need for climate activists, and then we took turns talking about our festival, and we invited them all to go. The librarians said they could arrange a van. Then we talked about the incinerator and how composting can cut down on the amount of waste, and Shawn asked if people would like to start an official club at the library.

Every single person there signed up and gave their emails, and they are planning a meeting in two weeks. It was a good feeling to know that there are so many people out there like us. One girl named Shay already composts and got three other people on her block to compost in the yard behind their buildings.

Shawn was so happy and relieved after the meeting. We all got Popsicles from a guy with an ice cream cart in front of the library and sat on the library steps with Shay and the eight-year-old, who ended up being Shay's brother.

Sometimes I think if we had won the Applefest grant, none of these other good things would have happened.

So remember, if something very disappointing happens, bigger, better things might be coming soon.

Love,
Auntie

THE FIRST RULE OF THE NORTH END CLIMATE CLUB

Believe there are people in every community who want to fight for our planet.

THE CURSE

Ms. Lane is here for dinner.

It's nice out, so we put Pea in her swing and bring our fettucine out to the sun porch. (Mom bought a little too much fettucine the last time she was at the pasta store.) Ms. Lane pours herself some seltzer and kicks off her shoes.

"I don't know if my body has ever been this tired," she says.

"What can we do to help you, Char?" Sarah asks.

"Uh. You're tired too, Mommy."

"Yeah, but we need to get you elected. Then we can all rest."

Sarah brings out brownies, and they start talking about knocking on doors and making phone calls, and how cowardly it was for the mayor to back out of the debate.

"The worst part is not that many people know he backed out," Charlotte says. "I wish I could find a way to advertise it, other than our very carefully written Facebook post."

"How about a letter to the editor?" Dad says. "I'd be happy to write it."

"Thanks," Ms. Lane says, "that would be great."

"How about the podcast?" I say. "We have a ton of listeners now."

"Oh boy, I don't know, Mary Kate," Ms. Lane says. "It's tricky."

"Charlotte, I think the podcast is actually a good idea," Sarah says.

"I guess I would only do it if you also invited the mayor to do a podcast."

"Gross," I say. "I really don't want to do that."

"Mary Kate, she's right," Dad says. "You would need to extend the invitation."

"He hasn't responded to the books I gave him."

Dad makes a scrunched face.

"Dad?" I say.

He stares down at his plate. "I figured I'd wait until after the election to get the box to him."

"Wait, what? You promised you would drop the box at Town Hall."

"And I will."

"I thought you were doing it right away."

I don't want to yell at Dad in front of Ms. Lane, but I'm furious. He promised.

I get up and calmly bring my plate into the kitchen. At this point, I am completely positive that fettucine is cursed in our house.

Sarah follows me upstairs. "Mary Kate, forget about trying to get Dad to do stuff like this. It's not going to happen. I think you should email the mayor and ask him to be on your podcast. Why not? You can ask him the same questions that you ask Charlotte."

"Fine," I say. "But tell Mom never to make fettucine again."

"What? Why?"

"Just do it."

THE SECRET ROOM

Rebecca texts **SOS** to the Bearsville group chat. Hannah is falling apart because she can't figure out how to organize the clothing swap at the festival. I make Sarah pick up Rebecca and Rabia and drive us over to Hannah's at eight o'clock at night, because it's a perfect excuse to get out of my house.

Hannah answers the door wearing a ballet leotard and Cookie Monster slippers.

"Bec, Mom made meat, and the whole house smells like sausage, and I can't handle your judgy face, okay?"

"Okay, jeez. Hello to you too," Rebecca says.

Hannah's house is in the rich part of town, where all the houses look the same and all the lawns are poisoned, flat, and abnormally green.

Her mom comes out of the kitchen. "Thank you for coming, girls. I assured Hannah she didn't have to do this alone."

"Mom, I told you Jay is helping me. But he's always at soccer tournaments, and I'm stuck doing his jobs." She turns to us. "Let's go upstairs."

Hannah's room is exactly like I pictured it would be. It's very pink and very neat. But I didn't expect the secret room that we get to through Hannah's closet.

"Whoa, this is so nice," Rabia says.

"It's a crawl space over the garage, but my dad made it into a sewing room for me."

There's a giant table with three sewing machines, lots of fabric and pincushions, and piles of pillows made out of denim.

"I had a new idea of having a swap shed in town," Hannah says. "Kind of like the Little Free Libraries, but with clothes."

"You really are a genius, Han," Rebecca says.

We sit on the floor, on top of piles of old jeans and jean jackets. Rebecca opens a glass container, and we each take a cranberry energy ball.

"I'm thinking of making these the main snack at the festival," she says.

We all bite at the same time and make loud *mmm* sounds.

"These are delicious," I say.

"Rebecca, it's like eating magic," Rabia says. "What's in this thing?"

"Just oats, cranberries, and a few secret sticky ingredients."

We eat the entire container in five minutes.

"Forget the fritters," Hannah says. "I vote balls only for the festival."

"Balls for the win," Rabia says.

It's getting dark, and we've done nothing but eat and talk about balls.

"Okay, I have an idea," Rabia says. "It's tickets. We check people in at the front table. If you bring two items to swap, you get two tickets to shop. That's it. Keep it simple."

"I've been trying to figure this out for days, and Jay's

ideas are too complicated," Hannah says. "This is it. Tickets. You saved me, Rabia."

"Hey, Hannah, do you still have your pet rock, Jacqueline?" I say.

"Yep. She's right over here." She grabs Jacqueline, the rainbow-colored rock with painted-on eyes, from the sewing table. "People think I'm strange having a rock as a pet, but I found Jacqueline right after my dog, Max, died, and I realized rocks are easier than dogs. She'll be here a lot longer than me, and she can't break my heart." Her eyes fill up with tears.

"I'm sorry, Hannah," Rabia says.

"It's okay. It's going to sound completely bizarre, but whenever I'm feeling anxious, which is pretty much constantly, I pick up Jacqueline and hold her in my lap and take deep breaths, and after a while, I'm better. I don't know how or why, but it works."

"It makes sense to me," I say. "I love rocks."

We take turns holding Jacqueline.

It's good to be here, but I have that deep pain inside me, the one that is always there to remind me that Lucy is missing out on things.

Hannah turns off the secret-room lights, and fairy lights come on, making sparkles on the ceiling. We lie back and stare up.

"Anyone here believe in fairies?" I say, surprised at my own words.

"Me," they say at the same time.

"Me too," I say.

Lucy texts me in the morning: **Meet me at the pond.**

When I get to the pond, I see Lucy walking toward me with somebody. I look through the binoculars.

It's Shawn.

"What are you doing here?" I ask, very confused.

"Lucy's family wanted to have us over for brunch to thank us for suggesting she see Dr. H."

"Aw. That's nice."

We show Shawn the bat house.

"We need a million more places like this in the world," Shawn says, looking around the preserve with my binoculars.

"There already are a million places like this," I say. "Lucy and I have plans to see them all."

"I want to come too," Shawn says.

"You can visit our eco-lodge," Lucy says. "We'll let you stay for free."

We walk to the pond and tell him about the hornet situation.

Shawn tells Lucy about his dad and the firefighters out West, and how worried he is all the time that a wildfire is going to swallow them up one day.

"That's scary," Lucy says.

"It's okay, because he's coming home soon, but it's been

really hard having him so far away," Shawn says. "I wish I had a place like this to go and sit. I sit in the corner of the greenhouse sometimes, but it's not the same."

Shawn skips a stone on the pond.

"Should we tell him about the panic room?" Lucy whispers.

"Really?" I whisper back.

"The kid probably saved my life," she says. "And he needs a place to sit."

We swear him to secrecy and lead him through the ragged patch of cattails.

"This is like a fort made by nature," he says.

"If you need a place to sit, now you have one," Lucy says.

We stare at red and orange leaves above us, and listen to bird sounds, and watch the squirrels chasing each other on the branch hanging over the pond.

It feels normal, like we've always been three.

I close my eyes for a second and say my intentions in my head.

Charlotte Lane wins in a landslide.

The Bearsville Climate Club Fall Funfest is a huge success.

Lucy is all better.

THE BRAVE KID WHO ISN'T IN
CLIMATE CLASS BUT SHOWS UP ANYWAY

Shawn and his mom and Sydney come over from Lucy's house with leftover pumpkin scones. His mom decides to hang out on the porch with Sarah while the climate club meets in Mark's band room to record our special-guest podcast. Shawn's mom and Sarah figure out they both studied psychology at UConn, and they start talking about their old professors.

Andrew Limski rides his bike up the gravel driveway and waves.

"Hi," he says, a little out of breath.

"Hey," I say. "Thanks for offering to do the podcast audio."

Awkward silence.

"I'm sorry you didn't get a chance to take the class," I say.

"Yeah, me too."

"Your parents didn't think it was challenging enough?" Shawn says.

"They say that was the reason, but I know it was because of my anxiety."

"What do you mean?" I ask.

We sit on the hay bales in front of the garage door.

"When I was doing the school strike in front of Town

Hall back in fifth grade, I was having a lot of bad anxiety about the climate crisis. I had nightmares, panic attacks, that kind of stuff. My parents thought it was because of the protest, but the protest was the only thing that made me feel better. I was only ten. I didn't know what to do. I still get panic attacks sometimes, and they didn't want the class making it worse. But coming to climate-club meetings makes it so much better. I think the class would have been really good for me."

"I can give you my notes, if you want. Like, we can teach you what we're learning," Shawn says. "And the club is pretty much the class now anyway."

"Thanks. I know some more people who want to join the club too."

"Hey, Andrew," I say.

"Yeah?"

"I'm sorry I wasn't brave enough to sit in front of Town Hall with you in fifth grade. I wanted to. I think a lot of us did. I just didn't have the courage, for some reason."

He nods. "It's okay. I wish I kept going. I'm thinking about doing it again."

"If you do, I'll come," I say.

"Cool," he says. "Why does Ben have a leaf blower?"

"It's a prop for Funfest. You'll see."

THE BEARSVILLE CLIMATE CLUB PODCAST

ME: I'm Mary Kate Murphy, and this is *The Bearsville Climate Club Podcast*. Today we are interviewing a special guest, joining us over the phone from Portland, Oregon. Climate Club member Rabia Mohammed will lead the conversation, since our guest is her cousin Farah. Please take it from here, Rabia.

RABIA: Thanks, Mary Kate. Farah is here to tell us about a very interesting program she's been involved in at her middle school near Portland. Thanks for calling in, Farah.

FARAH: Thank you for inviting me.

RABIA: Can you tell us about your Trash to Treats program?

FARAH: Yes. So our school started a cafeteria composting program a few years ago. We have a company pick up all our food waste, turn it into compost, and then come back with piles of compost when we need it.

RABIA: How do you use the compost?

FARAH: We have a huge community garden at our school. Every grade plants pollinator-friendly plants and vegetables, and we use the compost to cover the garden. It's very rich in good nutrients that help the plants grow.

RABIA: I love this. What do you do with all the vegetables?

FARAH: We pick the vegetables, and each class finds a recipe and prepares a dish. Then we all get together for a harvest party. And we compost the scraps. The party is really fun.

RABIA: Wow. That sounds amazing. I'm hoping we can do something just like this in Honey Hill.

FARAH: I hope you do. We've all learned so much from this program.

RABIA: Thank you so much, Farah.

FARAH: You're welcome. Bye, Honey Hill!

ME: Thank you, Rabia and Farah. If you would like to help us start a school composting program at Fisher Middle School, please come to our Bearsville Climate Club Fall Funfest at the school on Saturday, October thirtieth, from one to four p.m. It's going to be . . .

EVERYONE: *Epic!*

Dear Mayor Grimley,

We would like to invite you to answer questions about what Honey Hill leaders are doing to address climate change. Please join us for a live podcast, where we will ask you climate-focused questions. We are very flexible, and we can work with your schedule.

Thank you so much, and we look forward to talking to you soon.

Sincerely,
The Fisher Middle
School Climate Class

EMAIL FROM CAROL SMITH, SPECIAL ASSISTANT TO MAYOR GRIMLEY

Dear Fisher Middle School Climate Class,

Thank you for inviting the mayor to speak at your podcast event. Unfortunately, the mayor is otherwise committed.

Best wishes,
Carol Smith,
Special Assistant to
Mayor Grimley

Dear Ms. Smith,

Do you think the mayor would like to answer the questions we planned to ask in our podcast through email? We will read them on air so we can be fair.

Sincerely,
The Fisher Middle
School Climate Class

EMAIL FROM CAROL SMITH, SPECIAL ASSISTANT TO MAYOR GRIMLEY

Dear Fisher Middle School Climate Class,

Unfortunately, the mayor's full schedule prevents him from being able to answer your questions right now. Perhaps check back before Thanksgiving.

Best wishes,
Carol Smith,
Special Assistant to
Mayor Grimley

THE FRANTIC LAST-MINUTE
FUNFEST CHECKLIST

- ☑ Press release to local newspapers
- ☑ Climate-club member volunteer assignments
- ☑ North End Climate Club VIP invitations
- ☑ Tent canopies
- ☑ Electric-car dealer confirmations
- ☑ Compost company confirmation
- ☑ Gym setup team for clothing swap
- ☑ Fashion-parade model confirmations
- ☑ Food order for Rebecca's cooking demonstration
- ☑ Event signs
- ☑ Hemp clothing and leaf blower
- ☑ DJ Dizzy Lu equipment check for the fashion parade and dance
- ☑ Confirmation of Mary Kate's brother for entertainment
- ☑ Decorations
- ☑ Mr. Beam's book lounge
- ☑ Donation collection table
- ☑ Nerves, panic, fear of failure, fighting

DOOR KNOCKING WITH JAY

Sarah convinces me to go door knocking with her while Pea is sleeping on Dad's stomach on the couch. I was planning to go down to the pond and take a break from everything before the Ms. Lane podcast tonight and the festival tomorrow, but helping Ms. Lane win is more important than sitting on a rock, watching leaves blow around.

A car pulls into the driveway. It looks a lot like Jay's dad's electric car.

"Let's go. Our ride's here," Sarah says, grabbing her clipboard and the "Charlotte Lane for Mayor" doorknob hangers.

"We're going with Jay Mendes's dad?" I say, completely confused.

"No, we're going with Jay Mendes and his mom."

I open the back door and slide in next to Jay, who is crammed into the middle, next to a big box of doorknob hangers. He smells like really good-smelling soap.

He smiles. "Hey, Murphy."

"Hey, Jay." Suddenly, I'm wondering what kind of state my hair is in.

I have an overwhelming urge to jump out of the car and run to Lucy's and tell her I might be developing a slight crush on Jay Mendes, but I can't tell if it's him or his soap. My stomach feels jumpy, like the one time I took a gondola ride up a mountain in California and decided thrill rides aren't for me.

Sarah and Jay's mom study the turf map, and Sarah puts the first address in the GPS. It's all the way on the other side of town.

"Is there anything we still need to do for tomorrow?" Jay asks me.

"I don't think so. We have a couple hours in the morning to set up, so I think we're ready."

"Good. I don't want to get in trouble with Hannah again. It's like, I can't help that our soccer team keeps winning, and I can't do everything the second she asks."

"Are you good?" I ask him.

What a ridiculous question.

"At soccer?" he says.

"Yeah."

"I guess so. Sometimes."

"I never knew anything about hemp until you told us about it."

"I know it's random, but I think it's interesting."

Jay's mom looks over her shoulder. "Uncle Luis loves it. I think that's where Jay got his hemp obsession. My brother talks about hemp twenty-four hours a day."

"It's not an obsession, Mom. It's just a school thing, okay?"

"So why do you talk about it at home all the time?"

Jay looks at me and shakes his head.

We finally get to the first house. I go with Sarah, and Jay goes with his mom. I hear him from across the street.

"Hi. I'm Jay, and I'm campaigning for Charlotte Lane. Do you have a minute?"

The lady opens the door, and they start talking.

I don't think it's the soap.

THE BEARSVILLE CLIMATE CLUB PODCAST

EPISODE SIX

ME: My name is Mary Kate Murphy, and this is *The Bears-ville Climate Club Podcast*. Thank you to Molly Frost from the Honey Hill High Social Justice Club for letting us use her tree house for this podcast. Before we get started, I would like to remind listeners that our Fall Funfest is tomorrow, Saturday, October thirtieth, from one to four p.m. at Fisher Middle School in Honey Hill. Climate class student Rebecca Phelps will be conducting tonight's interview. Rebecca, do you want to introduce our special guest?

REBECCA: Yes, thank you, Mary Kate. I'd like to introduce Ms. Charlotte Lane, candidate for mayor of Honey Hill. We should mention we have also invited Mayor Grimley to answer the same questions we will be asking Ms. Lane, relating to how town governments should be dealing with climate change, but he was not available. Welcome, Ms. Lane, and thank you for coming. We're sorry the tree house is so crowded.

MS. LANE: *[Laughs.]* You are welcome. It's great to be here with members of both the middle school climate club and the high school social-justice club. And I love tree houses.

303

REBECCA: Me too. So I'm going to jump right in and ask you first: What inspired you to run for mayor?

MS. LANE: That's an easy one, because I'm sitting in this tree house surrounded by posters about unfair dress codes. Last year, I watched a group of students protest the dress code at Fisher Middle School and keep going until they were able to make real change in their community. I realized, if they can be brave and persistent in the face of adversity, then I can step up and try to serve my community.

REBECCA: Wow. Thank you for that. I know we agreed to stay focused on climate change, so now I'd like to ask: What could you as mayor of Honey Hill do to address climate change?

MS. LANE: To begin, we all must put pressure on companies to stop polluting. Listeners may not know that only a handful of giant companies are responsible for a huge percentage of carbon emissions. At the local-government level, we can put pressure on state lawmakers to pass climate-friendly laws, and we can pass our own climate-friendly ordinances, as long as we have enough like-minded people on the council to get the job done.

REBECCA: What would be some actual examples of things you could do locally?

MS. LANE: If the people of Honey Hill elect me, I will propose we install a microgrid in town, which would provide off-the-grid power for our town buildings, including Fisher Middle School. I will bring in grant money through foundations some of our residents are already connected with, to provide incentives for solar panels on people's houses. I will work with businesses to install more electric-vehicle charging stations. I will provide incentives to people who plant native plants in their yards and choose not to poison their lawns with pesticides and herbicides, which are killing entire ecosystems. I will work with schools, businesses, and local organizations to come up with creative ideas to raise money for outdoor classrooms, more bicycle racks, walking school buses, and zero-waste community events, like the one you all are doing. I think I'd better stop. I get too excited about this topic, and I could go on all night.

REBECCA: Those are such good ideas, Ms. Lane. As you mentioned, we are also here with the high school social-justice club, and Bea from that club wants to ask you a question if that's okay.

MS. LANE: Of course.

BEA: Thank you, Ms. Lane. Do you think it's important to talk about social justice when you address climate change?

MS. LANE: Climate change is a human problem, but if a tiny percentage of humans are doing most of the damage and entire groups of people are not given a seat at the table, meaning they are not in positions of power to make decisions related to their own communities, then the entire planet suffers. We must always consider equity when we are having conversations about climate change.

REBECCA: That's all we have, Ms. Lane. We are so grateful you took the time to talk to us and answer our questions. We know you are very busy. Thank you and good luck!

OATMEAL AND RAISINS WITH
A SIDE OF ACTUAL CONVERSATION

Mom is all nervous about her modeling debut. She's sitting at the kitchen table with a full-makeup face and curlers in her hair like she's going on date in the 1950s.

"You look like a babe," Dad says.

"Can we leave soon?" I ask. "I can't be late to help set up."

"Sure thing, Mary Kate," he says, folding the paper. He clears his throat. "So I wanted to say I'm sorry. I should have delivered the box to the mayor or told you I wasn't comfortable doing it. I stuck it on a shelf in the bookstore because I didn't want you to rock the boat."

"That sucks, Dad."

"Hey. Language," Mom says.

"I'm almost thirteen. Can I be done with the language police? There are more important things in the world than offensive language."

"Listen, I'm sorry," Dad says. "That's it. That's all I've got. I'm not as brave as you kids. I'm just an old white dude with a lot of learning to do. Okay?"

"I'll forgive you," I say, "if you let me say five curse words in a row."

His face turns as red as the ceramic chicken on the shelf behind him.

"I'm kidding, Dad. You should know I'm planning to deliver that box myself."

"You do that, Mary Kate. And *you* should know, I could not be prouder of you."

"Thanks, Dad."

"What he said," Mom says.

"Thanks, Mom."

THE CALM BEFORE THE BEARSVILLE CLIMATE CLUB FALL FUNFEST

When Dad drops me off at FMS at eight in the morning, Mr. Lu is in front of the school, pacing.

Dad helps me unload the pumpkins we picked up yesterday, and I wait for Mr. Lu while he talks on the phone with his mom.

"I'm not doing that, Mom. They'll think I'm weird."

"It's okay. I'm calming down."

"Yeah."

"Yeah. I'll see you at one, Mom."

Mr. Lu turns around and sees me standing there, trying not to laugh.

"I'm thirty-three years old, and my mom is still up in my business," he says. "Yay—pumpkins. Let the festival begin."

We walk around to the back field near the Kindness Garden.

"The canopies are already up," Mr. Lu says, "thanks to Mr. Ricky."

Ben and Jay are hanging hemp clothes on hooks next to Ben's leaf-blowers-are-the-worst table. Ben found two old barn doors to use as a display, and they've attached true-or-false questions about lawn machines and hemp.

True or false? Growing hemp uses less water than growing cotton. (True.)

True or false? Leaf blowers can cause hearing damage. (True.)

People start trickling in with hay bales and more pumpkins, and Hannah arrives in her neighbor's pickup truck, which is full of the clothing racks we got from that thrift shop lady's contact. She's wearing a hand-painted Swappable T-shirt.

"Do you like it?" she asks. "I'm working on the logo."

"I love it," I say.

We move in a group, like a school of fish, first setting up the gym, then the tables in the tents, then sectioning off the parking lot, just as the first dealer arrives in a matte-green electric car.

Elijah and Jay are in charge of giving jobs to the seventh-grade volunteers, who all want to join climate club.

Ms. Lane rides up on her bike, wearing jeans and the old sweatshirt she bought when she and Sarah took a road trip to Yosemite a *long* time ago.

"Put me to work," she says.

"You rode all the way here from your house?" I say.

"Yeah. You said zero-waste, right? Come on, give me a job."

"Don't you have to knock on doors?"

"In a couple hours. People don't like their doorbell rung at eight in the morning. Believe me."

"Go help Beam make his climate-themed-library-book-lounge vision happen," Mr. Lu says.

Our parents start showing up to "help," which basically means they stand around talking and making comments like "In my day, we all played in the dirt and didn't go home until the streetlights came on."

Ben's dad brings up how raking leaves is an art *and* a science. He looks and acts exactly like Ben.

I'm sitting on the bench near the Kindness Garden, drinking tea out of my reusable water bottle, when Ms. Lane walks over and sits down.

"Is the Beam lounge ready?"

"It's ready, and it's adorable," she says. "I'm leaving in a minute, but I wanted to talk to you before I go."

"Okay."

"I've watched you grow up since you were two hours old, Mary Kate Murphy, and I'm so in awe of everything you've done with Molly and the climate class. I know a lot of this is completely out of your comfort zone, and I know it's been so hard with Lucy sick. But look around. You and your friends are a force to behold."

Friends. The word feels warm, like hot chocolate on a fall morning.

"I'm proud of you too, Charlotte. When people ask me what I want to be when I grow up, I'll tell them I want to be a Ms. Lane."

She laughs. "Maybe with a Mr. Lu mixed in."

"And Mr. Beam."

"Love that guy," she says, wiping her face with her sleeve. "Ah. I have to get myself together. I have a lot of doors to knock on this weekend with my partner in crime."

"Is she taking Pea?"

"No, Jason's taking her to the festival. I'm short on Murphy family volunteers today because your dad wants to see your mom's modeling debut, and Mark is bugging Jason to watch his gig." She ties her shoe and stands up.

"His big middle school gig?"

She laughs again.

"Ms. Lane?"

"Yes, Mare?"

"I've been saying these intentions. If you want to try it, you repeat 'Charlotte Lane wins in a landslide' over and over again, as if it already happened."

"You know what? I'm going to do that. It can't hurt, right?"

"It can't hurt."

HOW TO FEED PEOPLE IN A MIDDLE SCHOOL CAFETERIA WITHOUT FILLING UP YOUR TRASH CANS

The biggest challenge of the morning is trying to keep parents, student volunteers, and Mr. Lu from eating all of Rebecca's cranberry energy balls.

"Who needs fritters," Mr. Lu says, "when you have balls." He pops another one into his mouth.

Rebecca is set up in the cafeteria kitchen with three seventh-grade assistants. They're all wearing hairnets and taking this very seriously. They have vegan pizzas in the oven and cranberry balls on trays, and they're stirring a giant pot of Shawn's dad's chili while Shawn FaceTimes his dad to show him what's happening.

"How are you going to swing the zero-waste part?" his dad asks. Shawn looks so much like him.

"We're using the school's trays and silverware, and compostable napkins," Shawn says. "The compost company will take away any waste we have today and compost it right away."

"That's outstanding, kiddo," his dad says.

"Say hi to Mary Kate," Shawn tells him.

I wave.

"Hey, Mary Kate," Shawn's dad says. "I've heard a lot of great things about you."

"You too, Mr. Hill," I say.

Mr. Lu comes in like a tornado and tells us his mom said there's a road race today, and what if people are busy and don't come, and we need to spread the word about the festival.

We're middle school kids with phones.

The word is already spreading.

THE PEP TALK MR. LU GIVES AT 12:45

"Um. Sooo. Like. Yeah. Here we are. A few weeks ago, we were a motley group of great big losers, unfairly kicked out of a grant competition and whining about it.

"But you didn't let me get away with boring bulletin-board suggestions—I'm looking at you, Shawn—and instead, you insisted we go bigger. You came up with a vision and conjured all your social media magic to get a huge crowd of people already lined up at the admission table.

"Look around. *You* did this. You used your superpowers. You made epic happen.

"You, my friends," Mr. Lu says, "are showing all those middle school haters who's boss."

"Thanks for being awesome, Mr. Lu," Hannah says.

"I'm only as awesome as my students, Hannah. Come on, it's go time."

GO TIME

Mom says she barely remembers her wedding, and not just because it was a long time ago. She always tells us that after all that planning, she was so busy greeting people and talking to guests, she didn't have much time to enjoy the day.

I'm trying hard to enjoy this day.

The first two hours are a big blur of classmates and their families wandering around and learning from Wayne Cress, certified EV specialist from the car dealership, about how electric vehicles work. The compost people brought actual dirt and worms and are explaining how composting helps reduce emissions.

I didn't even see Mark before he got here, because he's always late to everything, but now he's playing the songs I grew up hearing every Thanksgiving weekend when he and his friends jammed together up in the band room. People are sitting in front of him on blankets, and I'm pretty sure this might be the best day of his life.

Shay from the North End Climate Club, and her little brother, and some other kids from the meeting are here, and almost everyone brought clothes to swap. Hannah can be very bossy, but she must also be very good at organizing a lot of clothes in a giant gym, because everyone who walks out is carrying something.

At some point, Mr. Lu gets on the sound system that's connected to one of the electric vehicles. "Let's have all the models come to the main lobby of the school to prepare for the thrifted fashion parade, which will take place in the Fisher front circle in thirty minutes."

I leave Shawn and Sydney in the composting tent and run over to the back of the school to see Mr. Beam's reading lounge.

I'm shocked.

"Mr. Beam, it's so beautiful."

He put up a tent outside the library door and hung tapestries on the sides and the paper lanterns from last year's winter play from the ceiling, so it's like a colorful fort. There are the beanbag chairs from Ms. Santos-Skinner's office, and little tables with piles of books. All the beanbag chairs are full of people actually sitting there reading books and eating cranberry balls. And I don't know how he did it, but the whole place smells like cinnamon and cloves.

"I gotta go watch my mother embarrass me in a fashion parade," I say. "But thank you, Mr. Beam."

"Thank *you*, Murphy. You're turning me into a tree hugger."

"Aw. You already turned me into a book hugger."

"That was the plan all along."

OUT OF THE CLIMATE-THEMED BOOK LOUNGE AND INTO THE FIRE

Sydney's in the composting tent whispering in Shawn's ear.

"Stop. You're lying," Shawn says loudly.

"Nope," Sydney says with her hands on her hips.

"What's she talking about?" I ask.

"Um. I think you'll want to follow me."

We follow Sydney to the front circle, and I stop dead in my tracks. Mayor Grimley is standing there next to his wife, who's holding a **REELECT GRIMLEY** sign. They're both wearing jeans, fancy shirts, and red Grimley baseball caps.

"No. No. No," I say because that's the only word in the entire English language I can think of.

I walk toward the school, then back to the circle, then toward the woods, then back to the circle. I have no idea what to do with myself, or with my thoughts that want to be shouted.

You kicked us out of Applefest.

You said awful things at Applefest when you didn't think anyone was listening.

You accused our teacher of using kids to get elected.

You claimed our teacher was going to make the town "unsafe."

You used your deceased Black friend to make yourself sound not racist.

You ditched the debate.

You were too busy to do our podcast.

You refuse to even try *to understand how racism works.*

"Can you believe this?" Hannah says. "I nearly slammed into him on my way out of the school. He reeks of cologne."

My anger is swarm-shaped. My stingers are out.

I see Lucy out of the corner of my eye. She and her mom are at the electric-vehicle demonstration. People are starting to crowd around the DJ table to wait for the fashion parade. Shawn comes over, and then Ben and Rebecca and Mr. Lu.

"He's here," I say. "At our event. Without being invited. After Ms. Lane was working all morning and left before anyone got here, because she actually wanted to help."

The rest of climate class finds us, and Sydney, and Andrew Limski, and we watch Mayor Stuffed Shirt patting little kids' heads. We walk like a line of ducklings behind Mr. Lu, who goes right up to the mayor and his wife.

"This is not okay," Sydney says. She's half the size of the mayor, but she stands inches away from him and glares up at him.

"Okay, Sydney, I'll take it from here," Mr. Lu says. "Mayor, with all due respect, this is a school-sponsored event, and there's no politicking allowed. We're going to need to ask you to leave."

"I understand. Not a problem," the mayor says. "My aides had this festival on our calendar. They must have forgotten to check the rules. I'll head out."

"Have a great day," his wife says in a very fake-friendly voice.

"While you're here, do you want to do the podcast?" Elijah yells after them.

"Or the debate?" I yell.

They keep walking.

"The nerve of some people," Mr. Lu says. "Anyway, let's not let this rain on our actual parade. 'Cause it's fashion time."

Then we hear chanting coming from behind the old middle school building. It's faint at first, then louder and louder: "Let's go, climate club!"

Molly, Navya, Bea, Pearl, Olivia, Will, George the sophomore, and a bunch of other people from the high school are walking toward us, wheeling a giant mural on a wooden platform. The mural is painted on three separate panels, each with a different theme: compost heaps, clothes, and futuristic cars. It's so colorful, and woven throughout the bigger images are tiny paintings of flowers and rainbows and mountains and rivers and birds. At the top, in big blue letters, it says JUSTICE FOR MOTHER EARTH.

When they've finally wheeled it to the front of the school, Mr. Lu runs over and jumps up on the bench. He turns on a wireless mic and asks everyone to stop for a minute. It takes a long time and a lot of shushing for it to be quiet enough for him to talk.

"First of all, I'd like to thank you all for coming. And thank you to our spectacular superintendent, Dr. Eastman, and the Fisher staff, including our principal, Ms. Singh, Mr. Joe, Mr. Beam, Mrs. Tucker, Ms. Santos-Skinner, and custodian extraordinaire Mr. Ricky, for offering to clean up so the students can head home and get their costumes on for tonight's middle school dance. This dream team of educators is an example of what a stellar school community can look like."

Clapping and cheering.

"As I always say, the first rule of climate club is: 'The more climate healers we have on this planet the merrier.' And, boy, did you all show up to make things merry."

"I've never heard him say that," Shawn whispers.

"And thanks to Molly Frost, and our new social-justice club at the high school, for this extraordinary piece of activist art. Yeah, kids. I knew all about the surprise mural. See, I can keep a secret."

"First time ever, Lu," Mr. Beam shouts.

"I keep all your secrets, Beam," Mr. Lu shouts back.

Everyone laughs.

"I've gotta tell you, I didn't know what I was doing when I found out that I had been chosen to teach a pilot climate class. I was afraid it would be all gloom and doom and I'd end up with a group of kids terrified to live their lives because our planet is in trouble. But the truth is, after seeing these students work hard to figure out where they fit into this massive web of real solutions and seeing them grow and thrive over the course of a couple of months, I have never been so hopeful in my life."

More clapping and cheering.

"Anyway, don't ever underestimate the creativity and wisdom of our kids. And grown-ups out there, let's listen to them for a change. I mean really listen. They have the ideas. We need to support their vision, with our money, and our work, and our votes. And as for the Fisher Middle School climate class, stay tuned. We're just getting started."

THE THRIFTER PARADE

Mr. Lu hands the mic to Hannah. She clears her throat.

"Sorry. I'm a little nervous. Welcome." She looks at an index card. "We wanted to make sure all the families in our school community were represented, and we are committed to making this an inclusive event."

She gives the mic to Jay.

"All the models are wearing clothing that was either thrifted, borrowed, or found in the back of their closets," Jay says. "We'd like to invite you to take the 'no shopping this school year' pledge, started by HHHS senior Zoe Zhang. You'd be shocked to see how few things you need in your closet."

Hannah takes the mic back. "And now, please enjoy the fabulous Fisher models, walking to the music of our own DJ Dizzy Lu."

The models are standing in the school lobby, waiting to start the fashion parade. Hannah and Elijah run inside, and Jay grabs the video camera from the DJ table, where Mr. Lu is getting the playlist ready.

Dr. Eastman is the first model out. She's wearing a fuzzy electric-blue coat and tall boots, and she walks like a peacock. She's followed by Ms. Singh in a business suit and Mr. Joe pushing his dad in his wheelchair (they're wearing matching tracksuits). There are also a few teachers, and then Mom in her fancied-up turtleneck dress.

I stand with Mark and Dad and Jason and Pea as she walks around the front circle like she's a supermodel. She actually looks amazing.

There are high school kids, little kids, a three-year-old in a lion costume, and Ben's two dogs, wearing matching capes.

"Everything they're wearing is secondhand?" Jason says as they all walk by.

"Oh yeah," I say. "Hannah made them describe where they got every single piece of clothing. Nothing new allowed, except maybe underwear."

"Wow," Jason says. "They all look great."

Sydney comes out with Shawn's mom and Mr. Lu's mom. They're wearing evening gowns.

At the very end of our almost-perfect-except-for-the-mayor-crashing-it festival, I pull Lucy over to the bench next to the Kindness Garden.

"How do you feel?" I ask her.

"I'm okay. I've eaten way too many of those cranberry balls, and I really liked the electric-car demonstration guy. I'm tired, but I'm going home to nap, because I'm not missing that dance."

"No. You're not missing that dance."

THAT DANCE

Lucy gets to Mark's band room with her sleeping bag, and I wake up Mark, who's sleeping on the couch with his guitar on his chest and his mouth wide open.

"We have to get our costumes on, Mark," I say. "Can you go to the house?"

"It's my band room," he says.

"Oh my gosh, can you go?"

"Hey, I played all day for you free of charge, Pep."

"And I thanked you fifty times."

"I'm tired, Pep."

"Mark. You demanded my room. Go sleep there."

"Okay, I'm going."

Lucy's dressed all in black. I help her attach bat wings made from an old tarp.

"You look so cute," I say.

Mom found me an ugly brown dress at the clothing swap. I pin pictures of food we cut out of Mr. Lu's magazines all over the dress, because Shawn and I both realized real food would be too hard to attach.

I text a picture to Shawn. He texts one to me and writes, **Twins.**

Rabia and her mom arrive, and we take way too many

photos on the front porch next to the pumpkins. When school started, I never imagined I'd be a compost heap getting ready for a dance with Lucy the bat and Rabia dressed as an apple.

Dad carefully helps us into the car so we don't squish our costumes.

"Have fun, kids," Dad says when we get to the front of the school.

"We'll try," Lucy says, getting out of the car.

Now I'm nervous, and I don't know why.

We get to the entrance of the gym, and Mrs. Tucker waves us in. My favorite song is playing, and Mr. Lu is dancing from his "DJ booth" in the bleachers. People are hovering over Mr. Beam's quick-bread bar and cider table, and somebody dressed like a creepy scarecrow is telling me they want to join climate club, but I don't know who it is, so I tell them we'd love to have them and I run away.

The teachers cleared out the whole clothing swap and bagged up the things nobody wanted. Dr. Eastman is going to take them to the fabric-recycling place she knows in New York City. They even brought all the pumpkins and hay bales into the gym.

The lights are dim, and DJ Dizzy Lu is surprisingly good. It seems like the entire middle school is here, including most of the students from Hartford, who came on a bus Ms. Singh ordered.

I wasn't sure if I would feel like dancing, but I look at Lucy, and Lucy looks at me, and the bat and the compost pile wander out to find the other compost pile in a crowded gym full of fruits and vegetables, and monsters and aliens and creepy dolls and other creatures, and Jay Mendes, who looks very good dressed up like a hemp plant.

And we dance.

TEXT FROM SHAWN FROM A TENT IN ANDREW LIMSKI'S BACKYARD

Sydney had so much fun at the festival she now thinks she wants to go to Fisher Middle School next year, because she doubts boarding schools have festivals.

Dear Mary Kate,

This is the first time I've actually felt like writing a letter for this Ms. Lane assignment. I'm sitting here in Mark's band room, listening to Lucy snore because her nose is stuffy from all the dust in this place.

It's after midnight, and I'm so tired, but I can't fall asleep for some reason.

I want to remember how I felt this day. And how do I feel? Like we can do anything.

Mr. Lu was right. A few weeks ago, we thought not getting the grant money was going to be the end. But we really are just beginning. We're going to have more guests for podcasts now that a lot of people are listening, and we're going to do some fun projects with Molly's club. Speaking of Molly, I've texted her twenty times to see how tonight went, and she's not replying.

The festival was so good. We even got a thousand-dollar donation from one of the electric-car dealers because they sold four cars today to people at our festival. Everyone loved Rebecca's pizza and Shawn's chili and those cranberry balls.

Tomorrow is actual Halloween. I'm babysitting

Pea all day so Sarah, Jason, and my parents can knock on doors for Charlotte. The election is less than 72 hours away.

I'm going to stop writing soon so I can say my intentions a bunch of times before I fall asleep. My intention about the festival being a success definitely came true.

Lucy is here with me, and she went to the dance, and she was okay even though she had to rest on the bleachers with Rebecca, who twisted her ankle.

I might be kind of interested in someone, but I don't want to be like Ms. Lane, who wrote about her crush and then nothing happened. So I'm leaving you full of suspense, even though when you read this you'll already know if anything actually ever happened.

Okay, I'm embarrassing myself to myself.

Love,
Me

A HUNDRED TIMES IN A ROW

Charlotte Lane wins in a landslide.
    Lucy is all better.

MOLLY'S (PG-RATED) TEXT

MOLLY: Where are you? I tried to call you, and now you're making me write all this? I'm sorry I didn't text you last night. My phone died, and Danny came home and stole my charger. It happened. We watched two movies in his basement (both PG, so not actual horror movies), and I was sure it was never going to happen. Then he went upstairs to get us root beer and came back wearing lip balm, the Burt's Bees kind you and I both like. I could smell it. I thought I should probably go put some lip balm on too, but then I realized if it ever actually happened, his lip balm would smear on my mouth anyway. So the movie ended, and my dad was on the way to get me, and the basement was dark except for the creepy sinister goblin-looking decoration guy with glowing eyes they had in the corner. I ate a Hershey's Kiss, thinking it might remind him of the word "kiss." But then I decided to do it myself. I leaned over a little, and our lips touched, and it lasted like 15 seconds, and then it happened again, for like 20 seconds. Then we stopped, and he kissed my cheek and smiled at me, which was really sweet. In the car on the way home, he texted "That was fun," and I texted "Yeah. Really fun." That's it. SEE, I told you I would tell you everything.

ME: Burt's Bees will never be the same.

HALLOWEEN

There are things Lucy and I always do for Halloween. We carve pumpkins at Lucy's house. We make apple pie at my house. We go trick-or-treating, and we eat candy while watching scary movies we're not supposed to watch. These are traditions, and we won't let sickness get in the way of traditions.

So despite sickness, and being tired from yesterday, and being nervous for the election, we carve pumpkins, and make apple pie, and take Pea, dressed as a pea, trick-or-treating, and watch scary movies we're not supposed to watch until we fall asleep, and wake up on Lucy's living room floor.

I don't even care that Dad drives me home at eleven on a school night, and I'll probably be miserable tomorrow. It was worth it.

ON THE BUS

Lucy's mom said she overdid it this weekend and might not make it to school, so I'm surprised when she's at the bus stop earlier than I am.

"I'm going to try half day and go home at lunch," Lucy says. "Dr. H says a lot of his patients do that."

Molly sits with her, and I sit across from them with Will, who's eating Talia's Halloween candy for bus breakfast.

"Hey. Burt's Bees," I say to Molly, expecting it to be our secret code for *You kissed a sophomore for a total of thirty-five seconds.*

Lucy laughs. "What flavor was it, anyway?" she asks.

"She knows?" I say. I spent a whole day and night keeping this a secret, and Lucy knows.

"Cucumber mint. The grossest flavor," Talia says.

"Yeah, everybody knows," Molly says. "I couldn't control my own mouth."

"Obviously," Will says, smiling with chocolate all over his teeth.

Ms. Lane is taking a personal day because tomorrow is the election.

I walk into her classroom, and my whole morning goes downhill because Mr. Linkler is subbing again. He opens a can of soda and takes a big sip. He's getting comfortable doing whatever he wants, now that he subs for pretty much every teacher who's ever absent.

"Hello. I'm subbing for Ms. Lane today," he says. "I've written the classwork on the board, which is to finish the letters to yourselves or read a book, so please get to work."

I think I'm the only one in the class not writing my letter to myself, because nobody had time to do homework this weekend.

Shawn raises his hand.

"Yeah," Mr. Linkler says. "What do you need, Elijah?"

People look around. Shawn stares at him.

"What's up, Elijah? Didn't you have your hand up?" Mr. Linkler says. He's looking right at Shawn.

Nobody moves.

Shawn shifts around in his seat.

Ben raises his hand.

"Yes, Ben?"

"His name is Shawn."

"Sorry?"

"You called him Elijah. But Elijah is the other Black kid in our class. This is Shawn Hill." Ben gives him a look like, *Are you an idiot?*

Mr. Linkler's face goes gray, like all the blood has drained away.

"My apologies, Shawn and Elijah."

"They look nothing alike," Rebecca mumbles loud enough for Mr. Linkler to hear.

"Did you need something, Shawn?" Mr. Linkler says.

"I need a pen."

I hand him a pen.

I decide to write a letter, but not to myself.

At the end of class, Lucy lets me read hers.

LUCY'S NOVEMBER LETTER TO HERSELF

Dear Lucy,

Ms. Lane is out today, and racist Mr. Linkler just mixed up Shawn and Elijah, and Ben schooled him.

I'm almost finished with my Day in the Life of a Sick Tick comic book.

I don't feel great right now. Dr. H says I should see a doctor who helps with nutrition and vitamins and stay on the antibiotics for a while. He says a lot of his patients have to eat a special diet. He also says it can take a long time for these tick infections to get out of the body. The scariest part of the whole thing hasn't happened in a long time. I was peeing the bed and feeling like my whole body was falling apart. Dr. H says that happens to a lot of his patients, but I don't know any thirteen-year-olds who wake up soaked in their own pee. It was so embarrassing.

I have been worried about Mare. I wanted her to find friends, other than the bears and spiders. I'm so glad she found Shawn and his binoculars. They're like the exact same person, except Shawn is a little more obsessed with composting. Mare told me Shawn was ready to sell his great-grandpa's pocket watch for me.

I haven't cried this entire time, but I cried a lot when she told me. I never imagined someone from school would care about me like that.

Mr. Linkler is driving me crazy with his fidget spinner.

I don't know if anyone has ever thrown away their last will and testament, but I've decided to do that. I no longer feel like I'm dying. The tiny creatures infecting my body are dying. They're the ones who need (microscopic) last wills and testaments. Mare said I should throw it into the compost heap so it can feed the worms and we don't have to think about it again. I've decided to cut it up into a thousand pieces, and when it's a full moon and the fairies are out, I'll bury it under a tree next to the animal graveyard.

Mare will be there. She always is.

Love,
Lucy

A DAY IN THE LIFE OF A SICK TICK
BY LUCY PERLMAN

When I found out I had four diseases all from one tick, I didn't really think about the tick, because I was just glad to know why I was so sick. I've done a lot of research for this comic book, and while I hope readers think it's funny, tick-borne diseases aren't funny at all.

My grandma wanted to spray our whole property with toxic chemicals when she found out about my tick-borne illnesses. I know she wants to protect me, but spraying chemicals and destroying entire ecosystems isn't the answer. Chickens, opossums, and other creatures love to feast on ticks. Growing plants that attract birds who eat insects is a great idea. But, most importantly, we have to fight climate change, which is making the tick population explode.

I would like to dedicate this comic book to Shawn Hill, his mom, Gwen Hill, Dr. Denwood Houlish, and my best friend, Mary Kate Murphy. Mary Kate and I have spent our lives studying misunderstood creatures, like bats, bears, spiders, and now ticks. I hope you will take some time to learn more about them too.

AT LUNCH

Mr. Beam and I eat leftover quick bread and scroll through photos of the festival and the dance on his iPad. Neither of us feels like doing work on this day that's sandwiched between Halloween and Election Day.

"They should have let us stay home," I say.

"Agree," he says.

Mr. Lu really wants to "huddle and debrief," which means ask us questions about how cool his music choices were compared to other DJs we've heard.

"I'm in eighth grade, Mr. Lu," Elijah says. "It's not like I'm clubbing every night."

"Okay, let's table that, because I have news. Dr. Eastman wants to paint 'No Idling' murals on all the school buildings near the pickup lines," he says. "She texted me that from a corn maze last night."

We make a list of our successes from the weekend. In addition to everything going so well, and getting the donation from the car dealer and almost $3,000 from the festival and dance, we found out the composting company got so many people signed up for their services, they want to give our school a huge discount, and if our district decides to hire them to do the whole town, they'll give us an even bigger discount.

With the money we raised and the discount, we have enough to pay for our composting program—and over $1,500 left over.

"I have an idea," I say. "I think we should give that money to Shawn's climate club to get them started. We can't sit here and talk about equity without using our privilege to invest in other clubs."

Mr. Lu stares at me. "Not for nothing, but *yes*," he says. "Well, what do you think? Should we vote?"

We vote unanimously to give the $1,500 to the North End Climate Club.

Shawn doesn't say much. I know him well enough to understand that he's trying to keep it together. He pushes up his glasses and says, "Thanks, guys. Just thanks."

Everybody claps.

"Can we focus on the leaf blowers next?" Ben says. "It's getting bad now. They're all over the place."

By the end of the period, we've planned a Rake and Bake. We're going to get our growing list of climate club volunteers to go door-to-door, offering to rake people's leaves *and* giving them tins of Rebecca's cranberry balls with information about how bad leaf blowers and other lawn machines are for the environment. We're going to be raking and baking all the way to Thanksgiving.

I think Ben might be the most excited Boy Scout in Connecticut right now.

"Okay," Mr. Lu says, "I'm going to try to get through this without crying. I'm blown away, like truly blown away by what this class has accomplished in such a short time. I want you to remember these first two months of climate class when you're all grown up and doing your engineering or hemp farming or fashion designing or professional vegan chefing, or whatever else you end up doing."

"Eco-lodge," Shawn whispers to me.

"Stick together, okay?" Mr. Lu says. "Your climate club is your superpower."

The bell rings.

"Wait," Hannah says, reaching into her backpack and pulling out a denim pillow. "I made this for you, Mr. Lu."

His face looks legit stunned. "Oh, wow. Oh, this is . . . Oh, man . . ."

It says **WORLD'S BEST DJ**.

ALL SOULS' DAY

When I was little, I heard about All Souls' Day, and I thought it was the day souls followed you around trying to get your Halloween candy. I don't know where I got that, but I remember putting my candy in a shoe box, duct-taping the box, and hiding it in my closet.

That same shoe box is on a shelf at my parents' bookstore because my dad promised to drop it at Town Hall and he never did. So I'm doing it myself on the day before the election.

Shawn and I walk to town after school. The sandwich board in front of the bookstore is advertising what Sarah and I are calling the Clueless Old White People Community Read, and I'm glad about that. I'm still annoyed that Dad lied to me, but he keeps apologizing the way he always apologizes, with pancakes and invitations to "Come take a walk with me and the doggos."

We say hi to Ayana, who's helping a customer at the register, run to the office to get the shoe box, and slip out the back door. We stop and sit on a bench in the gazebo between the bookstore and Town Hall, and open the box. I take out the note I had written and slide the letter I wrote during English class inside the front cover of the top book, making sure it's sticking out.

"Can I read it first?" Shawn asks.

I hesitate because it's totally embarrassing. "Yeah, you can read it," I say.

Dear Mayor Grimley,

First of all, I am very sorry to hear about your friend's passing. I know that must have been hard for you. My best friend has been sick, and I don't know what I would do if I lost her. I hope your friend left you something special to help remember your friendship in his last will and testament.

I'm not writing about Applefest, because I don't think we will ever agree. But I have learned that sometimes accusing people of being racist isn't the best way to deal with racism. That's because you can have wonderful Black friends, or give money to Black charities, or say nice things about how Black Lives Matter on social media and still be part of the problem. My sister, Sarah, explained that to me, but it took a while for me to really understand it. I guess what I realized is that if we are not always trying to be anti-racist, then we might be contributing to a racist system without even realizing it.

I know I'm a kid and it seems like I can't understand these things, but actually I think it's easier for a twelve-year-old to get it because we don't have as much to unlearn.

I am sharing a couple books that might be helpful. I hope you will read them and maybe even go to the

community read talk at the bookstore. You're never
too old to learn. You can ask my parents. They're even
older than you.
    Happy fall.

                    Sincerely,
                    Mary Kate Murphy

"Happy fall?" Shawn says.

"Ha ha. I almost said, 'Good luck,' but I don't want him to have any luck the day before the election."

It's cold and starting to rain tiny mist drops. I hold the box under my backpack, and we speed-walk to Town Hall. The office of Mayor Grimley is the first door on the right.

"Can you give this to the mayor as soon as possible?" I say, handing the box to his secretary.

She looks at us suspiciously. "May I ask what's inside?"

"Books," I say. "I'm a big reader."

"Okay?" she says, taking the box and probably thinking it's a bomb.

I don't know if I'm doing the right thing, but I feel more like a person than a hornet, so that's a good sign.

No stinger.

Just peace.

CHARLOTTE LANE WINS IN A LANDSLIDE

On Election Day . . .

It's Sarah and Pea and Jason and Mark and my parents and me under a canopy with "Vote for Charlotte" banners and hats and mittens.

It's Lucy and her mom delivering hot chocolate in thermoses.

It's snowflakes, blowing leaves, and drooping faces on tired pumpkins.

It's the social-justice club on Main Street, waving signs, and the Bearsville Climate Club in front of the library, waving signs, and hundreds of people honking and cheering for Charlotte Lane, the candidate standing for hours on the corner near the polling place.

It's photos of Pea in her fleece bunting wearing an "I Voted" sticker, smiling a real baby smile.

It's excitement.

And nerves.

And joy.

And a win.

A landslide of a win.

For social justice.

For our climate.
For our community.
For Charlotte Lane, mayor-elect.
Tonight, the whole world feels like a poem.

WHAT IT ALL MEANS

I'm down to one intention, the one that matters the most. And I'll say it every day until it's totally and completely true.

Lucy is all better.

Mr. Beam throws a huge party to celebrate Ms. Lane's win, and it's as perfect as the book lounge.

There's a ton of food, repurposed paper lanterns, twinkle lights everywhere, and a very obvious honey theme.

"I like your house, Beamer," I say.

"It's Mr. Beam, Murphy. And thank you."

This must be what a hornets' nest feels like on the inside when all the hornets are relaxing.

Ms. Lane, our queen, is already writing people's ideas on a huge whiteboard in Mr. Beam's living room, with *Let's Build Community* at the top in perfect cursive.

"That's like the most teacher-ish thing you've ever done," Sarah says. "And you've done some pretty teacher-ish things."

"Hey, teachers get it done, my friend," Charlotte says.

Jay is here, still smelling like soap, still giving me the gondola-up-the-mountain feeling. I do not know what to do about it, or if it will ever lead to a Burt's Bees situation, but I will be calling a panic room meeting with Molly and Lucy as soon as humanly possible.

"Do you want to play Connect Four?" Jay asks. "It's the only kid-appropriate game Mr. Beam has."

I laugh. "Yeah. I'll be there in a minute."

The kitchen is loud and crowded, so I go out to the back porch for fresh air.

Mr. Lu is out here trying to finish his "victory playlist." He runs to help Ms. Lane's grandma through the back door and into the kitchen.

"Man, those tennis balls are a godsend on the walkers," he says.

"Hey, Mr. Lu?" I say.

"Yes, Mary Kate?"

"Thank you for giving me the chance to be part of the climate class. I know I'm not the best science student, but this is the most amazing class I've ever had."

"Mary Kate, you are the best kind of science student—curious, creative, willing to fail and start over, passionate about our planet. I mean, I'm the one who should pinch myself every day. You guys inspire me, and all of us, to try harder. I never thought we would be able to pull off a huge event with no waste. I mean, those napkins are already being broken down by busy little organisms. It's incredible."

"Yeah. It really is."

"I would have just said, 'Let's be lazy one more time and get some plastic plates,' and those plates would be sitting there for thousands of years after you and I are worm food."

"Gross. But true."

"Did you see even Beam is using compostable stuff in there?"

"I actually did notice."

"Keep pushing, Mary Kate. You're awesome."

"What's next, Mr. Lu?"

"Oh, I'm going to have a honeycomb parfait, or whatever Beam is serving in there, and maybe get a victory conga line going up the street."

"No, I mean with climate class. After the Rake and Bake?"

"It's a pilot program. You tell me."

I start sharing my list of ideas, but Mr. Lu is obviously more interested in his playlist, and I realize he probably needs a break from climate club for a night.

"I think that's a fantastic grand plan, Mary Kate," he says. "But first, we conga."

Dear Honorable Governor,

We decided Earth Day would be a good day to introduce ourselves. We are a student-run network of climate clubs. We started with two clubs in Honey Hill and Hartford, and now we have seventeen clubs, with hundreds of members.

Here's a little more information about us. Over the past six months, we have created composting programs in schools and donated the compost to community gardens. We have also painted anti-idling murals on town and city buildings and initiated leaf-raking and snow-shoveling programs to educate people about lawn and snow machine emissions. We are currently working on a vegan cookbook, with recipes that use foods grown in Connecticut. We've set up community sheds for clothing exchanges and are planting small plots of hemp along with our pollinator gardens. We have been traveling to the state legislature every week since February to lobby our representatives to pass electric-school-bus laws. Our sister chapters are doing similar projects, and every day we're getting messages from kids who want to start climate clubs.

We have done a lot. Now we are asking you to do some things:

- *Please declare a climate emergency in our state and immediately take the steps necessary to transition to 100% renewable energy.*
- *Please stop giving contracts and tax breaks to gas and oil companies and letting them build new pipelines that will continue the creation of fossil fuel emissions.*
- *Please invite people from ALL communities to help you make your important decisions. People have amazing ideas. You just need to listen.*
- *Please make climate your most important priority. It is for kids like us.*

Mr. Governor, you have the kind of power that can end the use of fossil fuels in our state and show the world how it's done. Our science teacher tells us this is a "big, hard, expensive ask," but humans have done lot of big, hard, expensive things. It wasn't long ago that the streets were full of horse manure and cars didn't exist, and neither did plumbing, or electricity, or antibiotics, or computers. People figured out how to bring these things to the entire world. We can figure out how to stop a few dozen companies from wiping out life on Earth (except maybe ticks and cockroaches). We have everything we need to keep fossil fuels where they belong—in the ground.

We had all kinds of rules when we started our first climate club. Now we have only one: Figure out your superpower, put on your cape, and get to work.

We will be with you, capes flying, until our vision of a healed planet comes true.

Happy Earth Day.

> *Sincerely,*
> *Mary Kate Murphy*
> *and Shawn Hill,*
> *on Behalf of All the*
> *Climate Clubs*

ABOUT THE AUTHOR

Carrie Firestone is the author of the middle grade novel *Dress Coded*, which was a *Booklist* Editors' Choice and was described by *The New York Times* as "a much-needed reminder that certain fights are worth fighting." She also wrote the acclaimed young adult novels *The Loose Ends List* and *The Unlikelies*. A former New York City high school teacher, Carrie lives in Connecticut with her husband, their two daughters, and their pets.

Learn more at carriefirestonebooks.com
@carriefirestoneauthor
@CLLFirestone